My Almost Cashmere Life

'Hope' is the thing with feathers—
That perches in the soul—
And sings the tune without the Words—
And never stops—at all—

Emily Dickinson

My Almost Cashmere Life

a cautionary tale

MARGY ADAMS

Paperback ISBN: 978-0-578-85166-2
eBook ISBN: 978-0-578-85167-9

Cover design and images: Eric Labacz
Editors: Rama Devi, Kate Allyson; Interior design: Tamara Cribley

Printed in United States of America

Published by Margy Adams
margyadams6@gmail.com

This cautionary tale is fiction inspired by true events. Most names, characters, businesses, places, and events other than those clearly in the public
domain, are either of the author's imagination or used fictitiously.

For all the Baby Boomers...

Author's Note

This is a work of fiction inspired by true events.

I am a Baby Boomer who was trapped between two worlds: a world of traditional values and an emerging, liberated world of too many choices. Coming of age in the turbulent Sixties, we 'Boomers' did not ask for starring roles in a twenty-four-hour lifetime movie, but fate hired us anyway. So many lifetimes fit into one, with no script and no rehearsals.

Like many Baby Boomers, I did not face life square-on, but was forced to by divorce after a lonely, thirty-four-year marriage. I began to write and write in search of answers and authenticity. In the process, I peeled back the layers and found me.

This fictional story inspired by true events is a cautionary tale, one that many Baby Boomers may relate to in some aspects of their lives. It is a story of loss and a bearing of scars. Through sharing, I've found that healing is possible and that hope "perches in the soul."

In the end, we each have our own unique story. I invite you to take this journey with me.

Prologue

Oh, Say Can You See

DIVORCE BRINGS ABOUT CHANGE TINGED WITH SADNESS AND RELIEF...

As I sit dangling my feet in my fancy hot tub, I glimpse the crescent moon in the pitch-black sky. An American flag hangs at a forty-five-degree angle, fluttering peacefully in the front yard facing my new cul-de-sac.

Four years before, I climbed into the soothing, churning water of my old hot tub and glimpsed at the torn and tattered American flag, waving at a ninety-degree angle. The flag was split in half due to an arctic winter storm and ensuing cold winds. The stars and stripes were attached by a slender thread, allowing Old Glory to wave in unison.

As I slid my backside down into the rhythmic jets, I marveled at the familiar setting. Above me hovered the nightly constellation of stars. I sank deeper into the blue-lit water and glanced across the Green River at the houses that had completed my landscape for nearly thirty years. Many houses had been remodeled, adding lit pathways down to the river, yet one house directly across the narrow channel remained the same. The static house had a small television that remained aglow for twenty-four hours, so I found myself staring across the river every night just to know that life did have continuity—life did have some stability.

My life had taken a giant step forward with a final divorce decree, signed earlier that day. I met this monumental phase in my life with a mixture of relief and sadness: relief that the marathon dance of two strangers had finally ended, and the melancholic music with the angry refrain had been turned down, but sadness, that two lives wasted so much time figuring out the delicate dance of two partners. We needed not only lessons and practice, but also chemistry; the music needed to be more joyful—more harmonious.

For years, I had ridden an endless dark roller coaster of resentment, not braced for the bumpy ride. I clung steadfastly to denial and grabbed desperately at half-truths. At the end of the ride, I reached feverishly for revenge but, staggering out into the light of day, I began to seek forgiveness.

Diving deeper into the swirling water, I wanted to blame everything on my ex-husband, but that would be grossly unfair. As I came up for air, I acknowledged that I had been frozen inside, driven by fear and unable to speak the truth. My desire to stay in a loveless marriage enabled my husband to trample all over me. Vast loneliness enveloped and consumed me—and went untouched because it remained undisclosed. He had been as conflicted as I, and we walked on eggshells for years.

How I wish I had stood up to him and demanded honesty instead of running off to play tennis. How I wish I had demanded we seek help, instead of opening yet another bottle of red. How I wish I had spoken truths, instead of stifling and stuffing my feelings deep inside.

Convenient and trite rationale kept me trapped. I knew no other role than wife and mother; my parents were married for sixty years, so I assumed that marriage was forever, no matter what transpired—blah, blah, blah…

After thirteen miscarriages…

And the surrogate adoption of my oldest daughter and the birth of the smallest preemie ever to survive—both of which complicated and blessed our lives—I stayed.

And stayed…

And stayed.

The "whys" still haunt me.

Now, four years removed from the fog of divorce; I ponder. I twirl my toes in the warm comforting water surrounded by a well-manicured courtyard and a dream-like house. *There are my two cats in the yard; life is not nearly so hard, so why in Hell do I have a need to walk into this writing class? Why can't I leave well enough alone?*

Maybe it's because we're all connected by the human condition of fate, and we hold a nagging need to share our stories in order to know we have lived. I believe life must be lived in forward motion, but life must also be understood from the rearview mirror. I have locked some drawers, sealed secrets tightly in the recesses of my mind, and now unlocking these drawers and digging through old files has become my arduous task.

As the Pulitzer Prize-winning author, my instructor, stood before us, he encouraged: "If you don't share or tell your story, it will be buried with you and in several generations, it will be forgotten."

That resonated with me and gave me the courage.

I am ready to climb nude into the churning waters of my new hot tub.

PART I

Chapter 1

The Deal

FATE HIRED ME FOR A STARRING ROLE IN A 'LIFETIME MOVIE'...

I was in the teacher's lounge during lunch when I received a phone call from my husband.

"Hello?"

"Hon, I want to have children." He coughed like he had something caught in his throat. "Can we discuss it over dinner tonight?"

I was confused. This call came out of the blue. I had just suffered my eleventh miscarriage in six years, alone, in almost routine fashion. I knew he wanted children, but miscarriages were my department to be grieved privately. I knew he was sad, but he would never discuss his feelings. Even after nine years of marriage, he remained a mystery that I couldn't unlock.

Caught off guard by the phone call, I wondered if he was having a sudden burst of empathy for our loss. Still unclear and a bit dazed and confused, I returned, like a robot, to my afternoon classes and took solace in the smiles of my seventh graders.

Balancing a take-out bucket of Kentucky Fried Chicken and a few sides of slaw and mashed potatoes, he barged in the door of our rambling ranch house.

"Can we eat in the den?" he asked. The den was a small room with a large fireplace, surrounded by shelves of books with room for one chair; not a place to eat. In the three years of living in our house, we had never once eaten there. I was even more confused than before.

He methodically proceeded to build a fire, while I dished up the food. He was acting so bizarre. The chicken didn't need to be cut with a knife, but the air did.

"Okay, I want to try to live with her," he blurted out.

"What?! Who?" I cried out in anguish. "Who is *her*? Who is this woman? When did all this happen? What are you talking about?" I was totally blindsided. He had been seeing another woman for months, maybe years, and I had no idea. We were so disconnected that we were living separate lives without realizing it.

And then, he began to rationalize as if presenting a lecture to his law students in his persuasive fashion. "I didn't mean to fall in love, it just happened." He took a bite of mashed potatoes and continued, "Living with her is best for both of us; I need to see if things can work with her. I never meant to hurt you, but life must go on. Please give me some time."

I sat in stunned silence. I watched as the glowing embers died. I was so unprepared; I was an easily influenced student. There was no mention of his baby, just love; no mention of our lost babies, just life and that we must go on. As if I had committed a crime, he set conditions for our separation. He asked for understanding and privacy.

I should have dumped the coagulated gravy on his head.

The next morning, he was gone. It was just me and the two Siamese cats. I called my parents to tell them we were separated. I made excuses for him, explaining he wasn't a bad man, just misguided. I carried on with my teaching and coaching, dragging home to an empty house every night. During the first few weeks, I unraveled the story and gleaned the truth.

My sister called a few days later. Alan had asked her to tell me his big secret: he and the other woman had a baby. I had no idea, but now things started making more sense. About a week before he left, I had come home after coaching a school basketball game, and he wasn't home. I sat at our square oak dinner table in my usual chair, staring across at his empty chair, and I began to question. Where could he be? What am I missing? Turns out, he was in the hospital with the other woman, watching his baby being born. What a coward.

Two months later, he came home. He said he was sorry and that we could never talk about this again if I wanted to make our marriage work. The other woman was married, and her husband threatened to take the baby if she left him. Since he was her husband, he had full paternity rights. She chose her son over my husband, so I was the default woman.

Sadly, I acquiesced to his requests. I wanted children, and my baby clock was running out of time. Alarms rang loudly in my head. I could not start over, so I chose to stay with the one who brought me to the dance. Besides, I now had a bit of leverage because he had been rejected and wanted to protect his reputation. I could call his bluff because I knew the truth.

He was defeated. He agreed to explore different options, including adoption, if I agreed to never talk about the baby or her again.

It was a deal.

Chapter 2

Whenever a Door Shuts

PIONEERS OF A SURROGATE BIRTH

As part of the grand bargain, my husband agreed to join me at an adoptive parents' meeting. We found our way to the basement of an old church where other anxious thirty-something parents were seated on cold metal chairs, awaiting the speaker. *Waiting* wafted through the room like a sad, familiar song. Afraid to make eye contact with one another, couples stared down at their brochures, pretending to concentrate on the philosophy and criteria for adoption.

In the early eighties, the Adoption Aid Society in our area was the definitive decider of who got a healthy newborn, for they were the prominent adoption agency and could call all the shots. They would decide our fate and set the bar. We were at their mercy. Every prospective childless couple in that crowded church basement was keenly aware of the competition and the slim chance of being accepted.

When the speaker approached the podium, she could have said, "All rise," and we would have jumped to our feet. As she droned on, however, my enthusiasm waned as I burrowed deeper into the brochure, fixating on all the impossible hoops we would have to jump through just to be put on a seven-year waiting list.

Even though the language was subtle, it was obvious that babies would be meted out to parents who had contributed most heavily to this Catholic charity, and who had agreed to raise their babies in a religious home. I glanced over at my agnostic husband, who sat passively with his head bowed. I knew the door had slammed shut on this option. We rode home in relative silence.

Whenever a door shuts… another one opens. That was my motto as I approached my doctors after having two more miscarriages. The fertility doctors wanted to help us. They wanted to solve the mystery of my inability to go beyond the first trimester.

Surely, not all thirteen fetuses had been defective, they surmised. There had to be a medical reason for my rejection of the developing embryo around the twelfth week. First and foremost, the doctors at the infertility clinic where I volunteered as a case study were research doctors and wished to advance science. That fact did not make them any less empathetic, but ultimately, I proved a curiosity.

Tests and theories were given as my medical records grew taller and taller, filling several binders. One theory was that my DNA was allergic to his DNA, and so my body rejected the union. Both of us submitted to a test for this and anxiously awaited the results. Nope, that didn't fly. Another theory was that my fertility had been altered by living downwind from the Hanford Nuclear Reservation, the world's first large-scale nuclear reactor of any kind. Hanford, contaminated by dangerous radioactive chemical slurry, affected a wide radius of communities.

My doctor theorized, "Improbably, but possibly, your fertility was affected by Hanford."

Everyone had a theory, but no one had a solution. I felt hopeless.

"I don't feel I can do this anymore," I informed my doctor. "I'm physically and emotionally done. I'm just so tired of being a medical guinea pig, and it seems like all the traditional paths are closed to us. Do you know of any alternatives? Can you help us, please?"

The doctor handed me a card. "I'm going to connect you to the Hollywood Hills Fertility Clinic. They've been successful with surrogate births."

"What exactly is a surrogate? How does it work?" I questioned as I slipped the card in my purse.

"The clinic has been running for several years and is the premier surrogate clinic in California. You will be matched with a woman who will have a baby for you, using your husband's sperm."

"Thanks, Doctor John, that sounds promising." I left his office wondering what the future might bring, fearful of what Alan might say.

The next day, I called and a very gregarious lawyer, who ran the clinic, took my call. He was a great salesman for these hot new "designer babies." It would be like the first match.com of baby mommas in today's indelicate vernacular. Intrigued by his sales pitch, I made an intake appointment.

We flew to Los Angeles, rented a car, and drove down Sunset Boulevard to Century City where the clinic was located. When we arrived, Mr. Lawyer boomed a greeting with a hearty handshake. He gave us a spiel and a few words of encouragement, and then turned us over to the psychologist who professionally guided us through the process.

"Margy and Alan, nice to meet you. I'm looking forward to working with you." She warmly clasped my hand. "Follow me to my office. Sorry, it's such a maze."

We wound through the hallway lined with Mr. Lawyer's framed law degrees, accolades, and awards. Pictures of him with Hollywood's celebrities peered at us as we walked by, kind of like walking by a *Mona Lisa* where the smile follows the viewer. *He is enamored with himself and celebrity, I thought. Glad we're working with her. He's too slick.*

We arrived at her small office, and she shut the door. *Oh, my, what have we gotten ourselves into?*

"Before we fill out any forms or discuss this process, I want to stress an important point about our clinic. We're not selling a baby."

Phew, it's not an illegal operation.

"Our surrogates receive compensation for their time and emotional commitment, period."

"Are you the only surrogate clinic?" I meekly asked. "You came highly recommended by my doctors."

"We are. In fact, we're the center of surrogacy and very proud of our record thus far. Celebrities are starting to use our services. We're very careful about who we accept into our program."

Oh, no, we're too normal. We'll never be accepted.

"We love working with couples like you. It's very rewarding. Are there any pressing questions before we start filling out these mountains of papers?"

Alan spoke for both of us. "I guess Margy and I have fears of rejection and concerns about the surrogate. She'll be the biological mother of our baby, so…"

"Of course, that's normal. Let me assure you that we have screened our prospective mothers and only accept them under certain conditions. They must already have a child or children and not want more. We've learned that a balance must be struck between wanting to altruistically produce a baby for a couple and wanting to do it solely for the money. It's a two-year emotional and physical commitment." She paused, but then quickly noted, "Our surrogates aren't flaky. They have the backing of their families and can backout for any reason. They're required to take part in a support group, and they receive individual counseling."

They seem like angels to me. The money allotted for all that time and emotion seems like a pittance.

The requirements to be accepted as a surrogate helped alleviate some of our fears and opened our hearts and minds to the possibility. "I'm going to show you to a conference room where you guys can discuss and process all of this before making a final decision."

For the first time in years, I felt like my husband and I were riding the same wave. We had a sense of we-ness for the first time in our marriage. As we sat together on the brown leather couch, just the two of us, we were faced with making a decision that would change the course of our lives forever. "Alan, I have so many fears. I can't take another loss. What if our surrogate just can't part with the baby after it's born?" I asked. "A contract can't really be enforced, can it?"

"We'd just have to accept the outcome, Margy. That's the truth." He paused. "Even though I'd be the biological father, a baby can't be negotiated by a contract. We're taking a chance with this clinic in good faith, and taking a risk with our emotions, but I'm willing if you are."

We walked out of the dark conference room, past all the smiling celebrities, and found our way back to the brightly lit lobby. We were ready to sign on the dotted line, ready to be matched with the biological mother of our future baby.

How can one explain the pain of unexpressed motherhood? I had been poked, prodded, and probed for so long, I was numb to the fact that I mattered. Finally, the Hollywood Hills Clinic made me an integral part of the program.

After completing the intake process, Whitney, the clinic's trustworthy psychologist, asked me to come with her to where we could talk alone. As we walked back to her office, I began to believe. She made me feel respected.

"Margy, I know you've been through the ringer, trying to have a baby. You need to know I understand your fears and feelings." I could feel her warmth and began to believe this could really happen. She continued, "I also know how excited you must be, but I'm offering you a perspective you might not have thought about." She hesitated, not wanting to burst my bubble. "Your husband will be the biological father, but you won't be genetically related to your baby. Right now, that may seem inconsequential, but down the road, there may be pitfalls. Just be aware that adoption comes with its own set of challenges." She paused, allowing what she said to sink in.

"Gosh, I never even considered that." I thought about it for a minute, and realized that it didn't matter. "I'm too excited right now to think about those challenges, but I'm really proud of myself because I'm the one who found you and this program. Without me, this wouldn't be happening."

"You should be proud. Few people have the courage to pursue surrogacy. This will be a life-altering experience, so just take care of yourself and your emotions. I'm a phone call away. It's been such a pleasure to meet with you. We'll see you soon, I hope, with a match."

"Since you brought up genetics. Can I ask how you match us? Is anything about me taken into consideration?"

"We try to consider your coloring and your stature."

"Really? That's great. Thank you, Whitney. This whole process is way more than I expected, and it's because of you. You've thought of everything. I never dreamed that my desires and feelings would matter."

"Without mothers-to-be like you, there would be no Hollywood Hills Surrogate Clinic. Now, get out of here before I start crying." She hugged me.

As we took off from LAX, *Waiting* wafted through the cabin like a gentle sweet song.

CHAPTER 3

The Door Opens

REALIZATION OF A DREAM

"Hello, Mom," Lynn greeted me from her home in LA.

I shot up from my bed, astonished by Lynn's greeting. I had been awaiting this moment for many, many years. "Oh, Lynn, thank you, thank you," I cried.

Two years had passed between our introductory meeting at the Hollywood Hills Clinic and this magical phone call. Lynn had been our second match at the clinic. The first one had fallen through because she and her husband decided they would never be able to part with a baby.

When we first met Lynn and her husband, Ron, connections immediately flowed across the conference table where we sat discussing the possibility of surrogacy. Lynn was the perfect surrogate. She had married Ron right out of high school, and had easily given birth to a daughter and a son, so they felt complete as a family. At age twenty-seven, this mother and housewife found pregnancy rewarding and empathized with childless couples.

As we sat together in the well-lit room, she discussed her reasons for being a surrogate: "Ron and I could use the compensatory money we'd receive from you. Living in LA and raising two kids is expensive." She turned her brown eyes toward her husband, as if requesting his support.

I glanced at Ron and smiled. He quickly took over and added an important aspect for consideration. Ron, who had been adopted, returned my smile easily. "I like the idea that your baby will know about both biological parents, even though only one will be present in its life. Although I had very caring parents, I've always wondered about my biological parents."

He sighed. "My parents didn't discuss the adoption with me, and I always felt different. Adoptive parents kept secrets back in the day I was adopted. Let's just say, I like the openness we are discussing today."

Such a caring man; he speaks from experience, I wondered what Alan was thinking, as I leaned in closer to hear Ron's sage words.

"Knowing where one came from is a desperate need for all adopted children." We all nodded our heads with this stark realization.

(Years later, however, I would pay a steep price for ignoring this wise advice. How I wish that I had made adoption communication a high priority.)

The sun streamed through the tall windows, adding to the warmth that permeated throughout the room. I enjoyed the two hours that flew by as we shared our stories, our expectations, and the actual process of creating this new life. As we parted with hugs and handshakes, I smiled from the heart.

With the advancement of cryogenic technology, artificial insemination was going to be a long-distance affair. Once a month, my husband would go to the donor clinic near our home and ship his DNA to Lynn's clinic where she would undergo artificial insemination.

After four months, the LA clinic called to report that only four living sperm were shipped, making it difficult for Lynn to get pregnant. We went to Plan B—we shipped ourselves, as well as my husband's DNA, to LA and went to Lynn's clinic, where he discreetly went in one door and, an hour later, she arrived through another to be inseminated with Alan's sperm.

We were out on the tennis courts, enjoying the warm California sunshine when a new life was conceived just a few miles away.

Lynn continued to be the perfect surrogate, who kept me involved. She sent an ultrasound picture and a heart-beat tape; she kept me apprised of her pregnancy through every changing month. I felt connected and secure. I revered Lynn for helping us, and she blossomed because she was the giver of dreams, the giver of hope and the giver of life.

Megan Anne flew into this world like a shooting star, arriving in the spring after an astonishingly short labor. She was perfect, all 8.2 lbs. of her from her round bald head to her purple feet. Her dad and I respected the birthing process and let Ron be with Lynn as we waited outside the birthing room in our white hazmat suits which the hospital insisted we wear. The delivery nurse placed Megan in our arms precisely at 2:01 pm, as a round clock showed in the background of our first family photo. *Finally, I'm a mother, and no one can take her away,* I thought as I gazed into her baby blue eyes.

Our psychologist told us that we owed no one an explanation about "what was going on" at the hospital. The caring medical staff were obviously confused on that momentous day, for I was visibly pregnant with our second daughter, finally keeping one in the oven. The nuns and nurses observed a young energetic couple handing over their beautiful baby girl to another older couple who were expecting. To this day, I see them bustling around wondering what the hell our world had come to as they prepared our daughter for her night in the nursery.

The following morning, Ron came with their two children. He carried in a big box of diapers and handed it to Alan. "From our family to yours."

Lynn, dressed in a pink blouse and white skinny jeans, walked down the hall hand-in-hand with her children and Ron. They stopped fleetingly at the nursery window. Their eight-year-old daughter shyly walked up to the glass and whispered, "She's cute."

The intact family proceeded down the hall through the double maternity doors and stepped out into the California sunshine to continue their lives. I watched the sunshine streaming in through the doors and smiled.

Chapter 4

Against All Odds

WILL THIS PREMATURE BABY SURVIVE?

After a whirlwind of friends traipsed through our house, celebrating the arrival of our daughter, I was finally settling in as a new mom. I sat with Megan contentedly, just us in the big ranch kitchen, lazily rocking. With Alan back teaching, I was enjoying my time with my baby girl. Five months from now, I would have another baby girl—a sister for Megan. Her name would be Paxton, which means peace. Life was good.

Within minutes of those pleasant thoughts and without warning, I began hemorrhaging from my womb. Blood gushed onto the floor as I screamed for my cleaning lady, who happened to be within earshot, "Shandy, help me, God, help me, Christ, Shandy, what's happening?"

She came running into the kitchen, grabbed a big white towel and shoved it between my legs to slow the bleeding. She took charge. She carried my five-week-old baby and me to her car, which was not equipped with a car seat, but she was determined to get me to the nearest hospital as quickly as possible. She wrapped a seat belt around us and sped out our driveway.

"Shandy, Paxton can't be born yet, she's only twenty-two weeks," I sobbed as Megan slept like an innocent lamb in my arms.

The emergency staff had worked their magic and stopped the bleeding but, when I awoke, the news was not optimistic. Standing over me beside my hospital bed were three doctors, neonatologists, ready to give me their plan.

"Your baby has a minimal chance of survival, even if we keep her in the womb for several more weeks."

I raised from the gurney, disoriented and afraid. I couldn't take another loss, I thought, as a second doctor bent down to deliver more alarming news.

"Your womb is an imperfect world with very little amniotic fluid, a placenta pulling away and dying, and your baby is malnourished and not active. But she can't be born yet because her lungs aren't viable outside the womb." The doctor's words pierced my heart.

I put my arm over my eyes, shielding myself from the bad news. I was all alone as my husband hadn't yet made it to the hospital; I had no idea where my baby Megan was, how long I had been there, or if these blunt doctors were asking me to make decisions. "So," I blubbered, "what am I supposed to do?"

"We'll admit you to the hospital on complete bed rest, monitor your amniotic fluid and vitals, and run the baby through tests to see if she's surviving." He flipped a page on his chart. "We know she's not thriving, but she has to develop her lungs. You're lucky that she's a girl because girls develop their lungs faster than boys." He paused and took a deep breath, letting that sink in. "I'd say we'll try to get you to twenty-eight weeks but, if your body or the baby starts to fail, I suggest you let her be born naturally because she'll never make it through the birth canal."

"What're ya sayin'?" *This can't be happening, this must be a bad dream. Didn't they want her to survive?*

"If I were you, I wouldn't want this premature baby born into this world because her chances at a minimal life are only 5%. I'd let nature take its course."

"What're you talkin' about? What does 5% mean?" *They don't think this baby is going to make it, but they want me to make the final decision.*

"If this baby's born before twenty-eight weeks, there's a good chance she'll have cerebral palsy, blindness, heart and lung failure."

"Please, stop," I cried. "I've made it this far, I know me, I know my baby…if and when she needs to be born, I want a Caesarean birth. I'll take that 5% chance." *I'll do anything to give my baby a chance at life.*

For two weeks, my doctors kept close tabs on Paxton and me. Every day, Paxton was rated on a scale from 1-10 for such things as sucking her thumb, activity, and amniotic fluid levels. It was a scale devised to test for the optimal time a compromised baby must be born.

As if we needed any more complications, Paxton was breach, already down low in the birth canal. Being an optimist, I believed somehow, since we had made it this far, everything would work out. I always looked at the positive tests when she was sucking her thumb, ignoring the negative tests that said things like she was limp, with very little amniotic fluid.

I spent several weeks in the hospital on bed rest and had horrific nightmares. Heartburn and heartbreak were my roommates.

On a Friday evening, my husband brought seven-week-old Megan to visit me. Dr. James was making his rounds and popped in to see us. As we were visiting, I felt a distinctive amount of warm fluid ooze from my body.

"I think my water just broke," I announced.

He surveyed the critical situation. "Paxton needs to be born tonight; her little foot is already sticking out into this world."

They wheeled me into surgery within ten minutes, where I was prepped and monitored. Lying flat on my back, I stared up at the medical personnel who were gloved, masked, and making haste. There were at least ten pairs of eyes staring down at me—a very frightful sight. One doctor started yelling, "The baby's heart rate is dropping! Go."

I felt a squeeze on my hand. "I'm here, Margy; it's Dr. Cara." And then my world went blank.

The doctor yanked Paxton Lee into this harsh world at 9:05 pm in early May. She weighed 17 ounces and measured 9.5 inches long; she could fit into the palm of an adult hand. She was whisked away and revived before they rushed her to the NICU.

I awoke in my hospital bed. Dr. Cara showed me a Polaroid of Paxton right after birth, and it was not a pretty picture. I felt a pounding thunder in my head and a volcano in the pit of my stomach. Fraught with worry, I was about to erupt. My poor tiny, tiny daughter was going to have to fight for her life, and it was my fault—my body had let her down. She didn't even have enough time to fully develop her ears, and she had one toothpick leg sticking up at a ninety-degree angle because she had not fully developed a hip. To add to my horror, she looked like an alien covered in blood.

After Dr. Cara left, my husband wiped his tears and whispered in my ear. "I saw her, I don't know, Margy, prepare yourself. This is going to be an uphill struggle. She's so tiny and her skin is transparent, showing all her blue veins. I couldn't watch her being revived, though they invited me..."

I rolled over and threw up.

Chapter 5

Believe in Miracles

FIGHTING THE ODDS

After Paxton's birth, I needed three transfusions, as my body had taken a beating. I was determined, however, to see my baby. Alan rolled me in a wheelchair through the maze of the bustling hospital. Before entering the NICU, we scrubbed and donned masks and gloves.

When he parked me in front of Paxton's incubator—her only home for the next year—I felt sick and faint. Lying naked, except for a doll-sized diaper, was an extremely premature baby with tubes and needles protruding from all body parts. Monitors beeped. The ventilator whooshed. I could not bear to stay any longer, for I felt so helpless, like a rudderless sailboat lost at sea. Slumping in my chair, I bowed my head and hoped for the best.

Alan took me back to my room where I would be discharged in several days. We would be going home without our infant daughter, an unbearable thought, but we had no choice. As we drove down the hill from the looming hospital, tears streamed down my face, though I took comfort that she would be in the skilled hands of modern medicine.

The next couple of days felt like I was holding my breath, waiting to see if she would survive. As a premature baby, her lungs were not fully developed, making it difficult for her to breathe on her own. She surprised everyone, getting off the ventilator after only seventy-two hours. Like many premature babies, her lungs were missing pulmonary surfactant, a Teflon-like substance that prevents the air sacs in the lungs from sticking together. In the beginning, every breath was a struggle. She began breathing on her own with the aid of oxygen.

Paxton bucked all the odds and survived with her sticky little lungs, but not without daily pain. Every day, the neonatologists needed to test her blood for oxygenation by pricking her foot for a drop of blood. Her feet looked like raw hamburger meat. It damn near killed me to see what Paxton had to go through day in and day out encased in her plastic incubator. I could not hold or comfort her because she could not maintain her body temperature out of her climate-controlled environment. She had a permanent feeding tube sewn into her arm, a Popsicle stick splint on her leg, oxygen tubes under her nose—and no one could give her gentle human touch. *She couldn't help but suffer from PTSD*, I thought, as I stood watching her day after day.

After watching Paxton get many needle-pokes every day as her only human touch, I couldn't help but wonder what would happen to her psychologically. How would we build trust with her? How would we bond with a baby we couldn't even hold? I had to shove all those fears and deep concerns away because I knew survival was first and foremost.

Within the first ten days, most premature infants need to have heart surgery to close a duct; Paxton was no exception. My husband and I were in the waiting room, anxious to hear the outcome of this anything-but-routine surgery, when we overheard two anesthesiologists discussing a case.

"How do you anesthetize a fifteen-ounce baby?" one of them asked the other. Alan and I looked at each other and knew they were referring to Paxton. He leaned into me and warned, "Margy, prepare yourself. Our little daughter may not make it; she is so fragile." I nodded as tears filled my eyes, but after hours in recovery, the little survivor went back to the NICU with a scar across the whole of her back. Today, it remains a thin reminder of her strength.

Within the first month when it was apparent she would survive, I placed two comforting items in her incubator. One was a miniature white lamb (which now has a prominent place on our Christmas tree) and the other was a picture of her toothless sister, dressed in a red sweatshirt, grinning down on her. On our daily visits to the NICU, the nurses would grab Megan and take her in a back room, eager to get their hands on a healthy plump baby. I stood like a sentinel, watching over Paxton, summoning strength from her will to live.

Upon examination of my placenta, the doctors determined that Paxton was literally hanging on by a slender thread. The rest of my placenta had no viability. She had been starving in utero, so she was far smaller than her gestation. In simple terms, she had a double whammy. She was twenty-six weeks gestation, but only twenty-three weeks in growth. At that time, thirty years ago, she set a record as the smallest preemie to survive.

Tiny Paxton was a million-dollar baby. We were one of the lucky couples who were not forced to declare bankruptcy because we had double insurance coverage. Over the course of two years, with months in the NICU and then months at a children's legacy hospital, the bills mounted. I threw them into brown grocery sacks and let the insurance companies sort them out.

Over the next three years, Paxton overcame many obstacles. The doctors performed one procedure after another; all detailed on the insurance benefit sheets that I also threw into the brown grocery sacks. She overcame everything from stage two blindness to Respiratory Syncytial Virus (RSV); she had a permanent feeding tube in her stomach, which burned an acidic hole in her skin, requiring plastic surgery years later. She had multiple hip surgeries over the next three years. Many bouts of pneumonia kept her in and out of the hospital and oxygen service for two years kept the bills mounting, but the incomparable medical care by the competent, tender nurses and doctors was priceless.

Each medical treatment added to our stress and our worries. We were traumatized by the process of one procedure after another, wondering if this trip to the hospital would be her last. We were exhausted, but we kept fighting for her. What else could we do?

A journalist from our local daily newspaper was touring the NICU and wrote an article that expressed something to this effect: "As I was touring the NICU, I was drawn to the tiniest baby, Paxton, who was no bigger than her daddy's teardrop. She was valiantly fighting for her life."

I often hearken back to those days and marvel at the miracle who is Paxton.

CHAPTER 6

Are You My Mother?

ONE "AW, SHIT" CAN WIPE OUT A THOUSAND "ATTABOYS."

Megan was only seven weeks old when Paxton was born, but when Paxton came home from the hospital for good, Megan was nearly two years old and used to being an only child. We indulged her like any new parents and immersed her in love, toys, and attention. But when Paxton arrived home, Megan's life was upended because Paxton needed constant care and attention, especially from me as her primary caretaker.

Big oxygen tanks sat in the middle of the living room, and Megan's playroom was turned into a hospital-like nursery, so all Megan's toys and play kitchen were taken out of her favorite room. Paxton needed 24-hour care, so after my day shift, a night-nurse would come spend the night in Paxton's nursery. She was a caring, beautiful black nurse who used to rock and sing to Paxton throughout the night. Megan saw all that special attention, heard the singing in the morning when she ate breakfast. She was so young that we didn't discuss in great depth why Paxton got all the attention day and night, but it must have been confusing.

During the day, Megan messed around the house with her toys and music and videos while I attended to Paxton. She had to be fed through a tube placed in her abdomen, and I had to be precise with the mixture, which was a combination of drugs added to her formula. No matter how much Megan needed me, I needed to focus all my attention on feeding Paxton in order to avoid giving her a silent heart attack. Megan learned to live with this situation. I had the luxury to be a stay-at-home mom, who was always present, but I wonder if Megan felt I was present for her?

Because a feeding tube had always been Paxton's only source of nutrition, she had never experienced food in her mouth or the bond of suckling. However, the doctors wanted her to try to eat, so we hired a food specialist who came to the house. Paxton refused to eat. We coaxed her; we pleaded with her, but to no avail. Paxton remained a silent witness when Megan, Alan, and I would eat our dinner.

A year later, having had some success with her eating, our family of four sat down to dinner at our square oak table. The girls were about three years old. Her sister, though only seven weeks older, was at least a year ahead of Paxton. Megan was doing all the things that three-year-olds do: talking, walking, and refusing to eat her food. Paxton didn't yet have a hip nor walk or talk, but she observed. I served each girl her plate of food and then took a seat. All of us began to eat, except Megan.

Paxton gave us a little smirk, as if she was fed up with her sister's non-compliance, and then she shoved Megan's plate closer. "Eat you dinna." Those were the first words she ever spoke, and she hasn't stopped talking since that day.

After three hip surgeries, Paxton started walking, running, dancing, and singing. One hot summer day, the two girls sat on the patio, drinking purple Kool-Aid. I could hear their laughter, so I came out to enjoy two little sisters, just hanging out together. Paxton looked up at me with a purple clown smile and started singing: "Kumbaya, my Maggie, Kumbaya, oh, Maggie, Kumbaya" while Megan tapped out the rhythm on the bricks. Their love and individual talents were on display.

Paxton became the Ambassador for March of Dimes and was on TV advertisements, becoming a celebrity who led the annual

March of Dimes parade. Professional photographers came to our house and took many pictures. Several years later, the children's legacy hospital launched an ad campaign by putting big pictures of Paxton on the back of city buses. Paxton pointed at the bus in front of us and clapped, "Look, Mom, Paxton on the bus." Megan was a healthy beautiful child and life was easy, but Paxton was the celebrity—-the chosen one, I suspect, in Megan's four-year-old mind.

At age six, Megan came running through the front door, sobbing and inconsolable.

"Why aren't you my mother?" she screamed.

"Oh, honey, what? I am your mother. What made you think…"

Megan interrupted, "Judy and Maria told me you're not my real mother," she blubbered.

Caught totally off-guard, I sank to my knees to console her. "Oh, Meg, oh honey, I am so sorry," I mumbled.

How does a mother answer that unexpected question when put on the spot? I hugged Megan tightly, but she struggled and ran down the hall. "Meg, honey, please don't run away, I have some things to show you," I said as I ran to the storage room. Rummaging through a box that contained Megan's birth memories, I grabbed a picture of her birth mother, the heartbeat tape and Megan's first sonogram Lynn had sent during her pregnancy. I handed all these mementos to Megan, who stood staring at me in disbelief, like the little lost bird who had fallen from the nest in the children's story, *Are You My Mother?*

We had not told Megan the unique story of her birth, that she was a well-planned surrogate baby, or that she was biologically her dad's, but adopted by me. The Hollywood Hills Clinic had cautioned us against telling her these facts before she could understand, and I completely ignored Ron's (Lynn's husband) wise words about being open with Megan about adoption, which allowed me to live in my 'perfect' world where I didn't have to deal with tough stuff.

It proved to be a big, big mistake, perhaps the biggest mistake I ever made as a parent, which wiped out six years of nurturing.

That night, I told her how she was loved and how happy we were the day she was born, and that she was in our arms right after her birth…blah, blah, blah. But I had failed her in a very deep, hurtful way. This omission by rationalization breached a trust between mother and daughter, and she gradually pulled away from me as the years slipped by. She clung to her dad, and began to build a tough exterior that I could not penetrate. From the outside looking in, we looked like the perfect family. But on the inside, we lived on the surface, always avoiding honest communication and confrontation. Sadly, we stayed stuck in our own narratives, building piles of resentment.

Brushing those major piles under the rug, life went on in our family of four. Unprepared for the emotional challenges our children faced as a result of their unique origin, our household swept unvoiced feelings away, adding silent clutter to its life.

Before our children were born, my husband and I never dealt with deep-seeded, unearthed issues in our marriage, so our communication never went beyond "news, sports, and weather." We seemed to have a secret agreement that there was no point in delving into our souls; better to pretend and put one foot in front of the other. Our children blessed our lives and caressed our souls, but our lack of dealing with their unique births with any meaningful discussion created a gathering storm that rolled in the night Megan ran through the front door.

I would be remiss if I only wrote about the storms and the dark days of our lives, for there were truly beautiful times too: simple pleasures, lovely laughter, holiday celebrations, milestones…it is just that one "aw, shit" wiped them out.

For years, Megan tested my love because she assumed I loved Paxton more. Through her lens, Paxton got all the attention, not because she was a preemie and needed me more, but because she was biologically mine. Nothing could have been further from the truth, but that's how she saw it, plain and simple—she resented me for not being her biological mother. Today, it is clear as a cloudless blue sky that adoption needs to be addressed early and often.

We could have avoided needless conflict if we would have summoned the courage to communicate, to share in the joys and sorrows of each of their births. Megan should have been free to tell us what it felt like to be adopted. Paxton should have been free to tell us what it felt like to be an underdog. Alan and I never asked either girl how they felt about their unique situations, so they never got a chance to tell us. Perhaps, we could have changed the family dynamic and had a better understanding, a meeting of the minds. We should have walked in each other's shoes… but alas, we can't change the past.

I see Megan, my little blond three-year-old, dancing in the rain, embracing life. I see her handing a rattle to her sister, patting her with love. I see her squeezing her kitties and squealing with delight. She had life by the tail.

Chapter 7

Gems of Innocence

GIFTS OF LIFE

Life is a gift we often take for granted. The unique way both my girls came into this world has made me look at life or actually face life from many perspectives. When Megan was born, I never considered that not being her biological parent would ever matter. I was naively mistaken. Up until age six, life with Megan was pure joy; everything about parenthood was new and exciting. On the other hand, when Paxton was born, life became overwhelming. Did I dare fall in love with my premature infant who didn't even have developed ears?

But I fell hard for Paxton and when she joined our family permanently, we were off and running, ready to live life to its fullest, creating traditions and memories to last a lifetime.

When the girls were four years old, we took them to Disneyland in Los Angeles and then to SeaWorld in San Diego. For two days, they were immersed in the Magic Kingdom of Mickey and Minnie. They danced with Cinderella; they were in ToonTown; they were in heaven. On the third day, we drove several hours to San Diego, excited to show them the magic of dolphins and whales. Alan and Megan were walking hand-in-hand ahead of Paxton and me. I had Paxton ensconced in a wagon shaped like Shamu, the killer whale. I was pulling her from one show to another, and half-way in between, she screamed, "Goddammit! where are Mickey and Minnie?" Out of the mouths of babes, memories are made.

My brother's children and my girls have been close since they were born. When they were just babies and for the next fifteen years, my brother's children, Joey, Sophia, and Brittney, joined with Megan and Paxton like a pack, celebrating birthdays, holidays, and vacations together. During the summer, my girls would go to their cousins' home in the 'land of greens' called the Palouse. The Missoula floods of the ice age had washed over the land, ultimately creating fine loess soil, perfect for growing spring and winter wheat, the lifeblood of the region in southeastern Washington. I captured a picture of the five kids, holding hands in mid-air, mid-jump above a trampoline with the green-covered rolling hills in the background. The cousins lived high on a hill in the country, close to the family farm, and my girls' visits always included a ride on my brother's tractor and huge harvester. The kids rode horses and 4-wheelers into the tiny town where there were more dogs and cats than people.

When their family came to Seattle, we would give them the city tour, starting with a trip to Pike Place Market. Joey would always ask, "Can we go see the flying fish?" Pike's fishmongers are famous for tossing slimy, bug-eyed fish through the air to another fishmonger who catches it and wraps it before giving it to the cus-tomer. The market is awash with colorful flower booths, exotic fish displays and Pacific Northwest crafts. The smell of ethnic foods wafts throughout the Market, leaving all visitors with an indelible memory. Before leaving Pike's Market, we would wind our way below to an unassuming alleyway to a brick wall covered in used chewing gum. People have been sticking their colorful wad of gum on this wall since the early 1990's, and one could smell the mint, sugary scent before rounding the corner to face the gum wall. The kids were fas-cinated and grossed-out at the same time. Lifetime memories were made, and although they are all grown with families of their own, they remain close.

Every summer, we also went with my brother's family for a vacation in Sun Valley. Joey, Megan, Sophia, and even young Brittney could swim circles around Paxton, ride big bikes and ice-skate with reckless abandon. Because Paxton's thick glasses were her lifeline, swimming and diving were problematic. The kids all decided they would dive off the springboard. Joey, who was six, climbed up on the board and took a flying jump, making a cannon-ball splash. Megan walked cautiously to the end, put her hands in a 'V' and dove daintily into the water, garnering an acceptable attempt. Sophia, who was four, like Megan and Paxton, did the same. Next came two-year-old Brittney, a natural born athlete. She took off running, doing a spring-board jump, and dove like an Olympian under the water with 'nary a splash.

Then came Paxton, swinging her Barbie doll as she walked to the end of the plank. She threw Barbie high in the air, and Barbie did her diving. Handling life in her own fashion, she took a bow, walked down the ladder of the diving board and fished Barbie from the pool.

One year we took my parents along on our annual trip to Sun Valley. By this time, Paxton could ride her bike with the others, but her bike was without gears. On a clear-blue cloudless day, the kids decided they wanted to ride their bikes into Ketchum, the small center of the Sun Valley resort area. Coming back up a long hill was a mile-long climb, no small feat for a bike with no gears. All the kids arrived at the top of the hill before Paxton, but pretty soon, she came along, pumping her little legs like a windmill.

My dad was waiting with me at the top, and started clapping when he saw her, so proud and impressed by her determination. "Well, Pax, the Max, how'd you ever make it up that hill?"

She climbed off her bike, took off her helmet and looked up at her grandfather. "Well, Papa, if you don't keep going, you'll never get there." He never forgot that for the rest of his life.

Through Paxton's triumphs, she has shown me how to face and accept challenges and how to persevere down the long corridor of life. With Megan, I have, sadly, walked a different corridor, and I am still learning how our paths could have diverged from one another so drastically when her childhood had been so idyllic.

Megan was the golden girl, destined to be a dancer. I noticed this by age two as she would dress in glitzy costumes, complete with red patent shoes, and tap on our wooden floors. On her third birthday, she stood outside in her party dress under the covered patio in a downpour and danced like Gene Kelly, singing in the rain. I enrolled her in dance classes where she became the premier dancer in every age group. Through the years there were special performances, one where she was on pointe by fifth grade and danced with the Sesame Street troupe that had come to Seattle. I was a chaperone for her dance company that toured Japan for several weeks. My blonde dancer, who was a young teen, attracted attention wherever she danced. After one performance on a grand stage in Tokyo, the host family's dad approached me and whispered in broken English, "Megan best dancer." I was one proud mom and those memories of my beautiful dancer often float through my head.

Where Megan was the dancer, Paxton was the singer, but when most kids were listening to Raffi and singing *The Wheels on the Bus*, Paxton was belting out Patsy Cline songs. When she was six, Paxton went to her pediatrician for a check-up. The doctor asked her, "What's your favorite song?"

"Crazy, I'm crazy for feelin' so lonely," Paxton belted out, imitating Patsy Cline. "I'm crazy, crazy for feelin' so blue." The pediatrician cracked a huge smile and memorialized it on her chart.

As the years went by, Paxton caught up with her peers. When one is born so prematurely, there is a lot of catching-up to do. She has always marched to her own tune and is a little quirky, but she is graced with an old soul and is happier than most young adults because she has inner strength from overcoming so many obstacles.

That inner strength served her well when Alan and I went through a contentious divorce. She had turned 21 and became the only adult in our house. Megan was away at college. I was naive and desperate to save our marriage, so I did whatever my husband wanted. Since he was desperate to hide the truth, unable to ask for a divorce because of financial malfeasance, he needed to gamble. He needed action. He was always asking me to go to the Indian casinos or to go with him to Las Vegas.

Paxton confronted me one evening and asked, "Mom, what are you doing?"

I curtly replied, "Well, Pax, sometimes you have to compromise in a marriage."

"Mom, compromise means give and take. He does all the taking, and you do all the giving." She put her hands on her hips and continued, "What you're doing is compromising your values." She turned and walked out of the room.

As the years have gone by, Paxton has stayed connected and grown closer to her dad, but she has never gotten closure in the way she has with me. We talk about everything, and I have asked for and received forgiveness for what I put my girls through. He, on the other hand, can only talk news, sports, weather, and dogs. So, I posed this question to her: "What's your secret?"

She smiled. "Lower your expectations."

Chapter 8

Spanky and His Gang

A TRIBUTE TO MY LIFETIME DOG; A SPECIAL BOND.

When Megan and Paxton were in junior high, our lives dramatically changed when we brought a new puppy into our family. None of us ever imagined the impact a dog we named Spanky would have on our lives.

Our old Golden Retriever, Jack, had been Megan and Paxton's childhood companion, but he had been failing over the last couple of months, so they asked if we would consider getting a puppy. On a dark and rainy February night, Megan, Paxton, and I drove over an hour on a winding, country road to a farm to "just take a peek" at the puppies we saw advertised in the classified ads. When we finally arrived after many missed turns, one puppy after another was leaving with its new owner—a black one, a yellow one, a red one. The eleven puppies advertised were now down to only three. Just as one gets caught up in a frenzied fire sale, my girls and I immediately decided we had to have one.

We held our potential long-haired, red one in our arms, mulling over short-hair versus long-hair. He was sweet and docile, but soon

41

we noticed that his little black nose was only half-there. Although we felt rather lousy, we wanted to look at another who wasn't defective. Laying the innocent puppy back in its bed, we picked up the handsome, short-haired, red one who had cocked his head and wagged his tail as if to say, "Look at me." Instantly, we knew he was the one. We also had a hunch he had been the puppy that had bitten the nose of his brother in a playful puppy romp.

We paid $50 to cover his shots, and then we walked out the door, leaving his Golden Retriever mother behind. She did not seem to care that her puppies were being carted off, for she was comfortably ensconced in her home with her human family. Her job as a mother was done.

The minute we put our squirming, licking puppy in the car, he became family.

This handsome, short-haired, red dog with gigantic paws needed a name. Since it was February, Megan suggested Cupid. "Really? Does this puppy look like a Cupid to you?" I inquired, as I was picking-up the second chewed-up pillow of the day. "He's a wild-child with too much attitude for a Cupid."

Murphy, Dusty, Big Red, on and on the suggestions came until we glanced at the TV movie just starting, a modern remake of *Spanky and Our Gang*. "How about Spanky?" I proposed, and it stuck, fitting him like a glove.

Alan called him "Da Man" and, as it turned out, Spanky was the most loving consistent man in my life, never wavering in his devotion.

As my big red dog and I walked the path along the Green River, a middle-aged woman stopped abruptly in front of us, bent down and patted Spanky on the head, "What kind of dog is he?" she asked.

My stock answer to that oft-asked question was: "He is half Golden Retriever and half 'Who's-yer-daddy.'"

"What kind of breed is 'Who's-yer-daddy'?" She asked in an inquisitive way like she really wanted to know. Not wanting to embarrass her by explaining or drawing out 'Who-is-your-daddy', I smiled and my best friend and I ambled on.

Spanky, also known as the Spankmeister, loved us, but he also had a long enduring love affair with tennis balls. He chased them, he ate them, he coveted them, and he hid them. He stole them from other dogs in the park and at the lake. He stole them from people in the middle of a tennis game, breaking through the unlatched gate at the court's entrance. If I walked in the door with my tennis bag, he would lunge at the bag, unzip it, and grab the balls. He mastered having two balls in his mouth at one time; he worked on getting three, but settled for two with another between his paws.

He did not play fair. He loved his version of playing ball: He would rush down the hill after a thrown ball, but he would stand stubbornly at the bottom, quivering, waiting for the second. When he finally came back up the hill, he would plop down at our feet, cradling both balls between his paws, but when we tried to pry them loose, he would lower his head to his paws, clamping down harder. If we ignored him, he would cry.

Paxton played tennis in our driveway, hitting against a green wall we had fashioned out of plywood. Spanky insisted on standing in front of the green wall, retrieving every ball my daughter hit. It became a game to him, but an annoying problem for Paxton. After jumping up and grabbing a fifty-mile per hour forehand before it smacked against the wall, Spanky would run off with the ball. She tried to outsmart him by always having two balls. She would hit, he would grab, and spit out the first as the second came zinging in. Then there would be a mad scramble to get both balls before Spanky put them in his mouth, refusing to give them back. She finally got exasperated, leaving him inside whenever she wanted to hit. Unfortunately, that plan was ineffective because Spanky could open every door in our rambling ranch house, and the minute he heard the whack of the ball hitting against the wall, he was out the door.

Spanky also had his neighborhood friends. At first, Spanky was invited to join me at my neighbors to have a romp with Harry, my neighbor's Golden-Doodle. But Spanky became obsessed with Harry's stuffed-animal toys. He would run off with them and start ripping them apart. There's nothing crazier-looking than two fifty-something women chasing after a mischievous dog with a big stuffed duck in his mouth.

"Spanky, get back here right now," I would shriek. He had considered it another game and dodged and darted all around the yard.

After that, Spanky had been specifically uninvited, so, whenever I went to the neighbor's, I would sneak down the driveway before Spanky could figure out where I was going. Sometimes, he would beat me there—the smart rascal—and be in her family room choosing his favorite toy from a big wicker basket.

One day Wendy lamented, "Harry's favorite mallard duck is missing. Do you think Spanky has it?"

"Gee, Wendy, I'll check, but I haven't seen it with his other toys."

A few weeks later as I was working in the yard, Spanky was digging near the pond. In his mouth was Harry's favorite mallard duck. I could not believe this dog's thought process. He had been burying Harry's duck, but once every few days he would move it to another hole. I made eye contact with him just as he was pulling the colorful duck from its latest hole. He gave me that "if looks could kill" look, and we both went about our prospective business. To this day, I have not told Wendy that yes, indeed, Spanky had stolen Harry's favorite stuffed animal. Some things are just too amazing to explain.

A year later, Tucker, a six-week-old tri-colored Shih-Tzu, joined our family. In August, a few months later, two gray tabbies, a brother and sister rescued from my brother's farm came to live with us. Spanky's gang was complete.

Although Tucker had been terrified the first night that he saw Spanky and had hidden behind a bookshelf in Paxton's bedroom, they became inseparable. Spanky became Tucker's everything: his nursemaid, his playmate, his boss, and his sleeping buddy. When we walked them, they made quite a pair, garnering many questions, comments, and smiles. Spanky and Tucker were like Yogi and Boo-Boo; in fact, we often wished we had named them such.

Tucker, who had been weaned too soon, would suck on Spanky's ears daily. Truth be told, the sucking was soothing for Spanky as well. Tucker loved to play tug-of-war with a towel. Prancing up to Spanky, he would shove the towel up to Spanky's mouth, enticing him to grab hold. Spanky could have snatched the towel from Tuck in a hot second, but he always played along, allowing Tucker hours of entertainment.

When it came to Spanky's tennis balls, however, that was a different story. Tucker would work hard to get his mouth around a tennis ball, snagging it with his little pointy teeth, and then he would run up to Spanky, shoving the ball in his mouth. Spanky would snatch the slobbery ball instantly from Tuck's mouth. Over the next ten years, Tucker would attempt this on a daily basis. In my estimation, Spanky had not been far-removed from his wolf ancestors in intelligence and survival instincts, but Tucker, who had been bred to fit into the sleeve of the Chinese Emperor, had been far removed; it's hard to fathom they were from the same canine species.

One Christmas, my parents stayed with us, so Alan really put on the dog for them. He wrapped six filet mignons in slightly cooked bacon, seasoned them to perfection and then put them outside near the barbecue to get them room temperature while we had our cocktails inside. An hour later, Alan walked out the sliding glass door, wondering why it was already open.

Cowering in the dirt at the corner of the house with his head bowed sat Spanky, who would not make eye contact with Alan.

"What's the matter, Spanks?" He soon learned the answer to that question. An empty pan sat next to the barbecue, and we settled for salad and all the trimmings that Christmas Eve night. That was the first and last Christmas Eve that our big red dog was not allowed underneath the table waiting for his usual scraps after the feast.

Spanky loved road trips in my Jeep Cherokee where he rode sitting in the back seat as if he were human. His hind legs would rest on the middle hump, and he would thrust his massive head forward, like he was riding shotgun. Often, he would rest his head on my shoulder. Spanky had always been keenly aware of his surroundings. He knew where we were headed, yelping and whining as we took the last turn to our destination. He knew the short trips, the mundane trips, the familiar trips, the ones to the grocery store, the vet, the bank—but he also knew when he was in for the long haul on his favorite trips to the beach and our yearly trip to Sun Valley.

Probably his favorite, however, were his trips to the Dairy Queen where he and Tucker would get their doggy cones. We would pull up to the drive-thru and, by that time, Spanky would be hootin' and hollerin' so loudly I could barely hear the speakerphone. Somehow, we would manage to get our order and proceed to the window. Spanky could not contain himself and, as the server passed the cones to me, he would intercept the pass, snapping both his and Tuck's cones from the server's hand. He would gobble them within seconds. The servers were always amused, as was I. I would get my swirl cone and, before pulling away, Spanky would always sneak a lick. It was just part of the deal.

Spanky and his gang added to the chaos of our lives, but they were an enduring and integral part of our lives at our Woodhaven home. When it was time to move on, Spanky moved on with me and our bond became stronger.

Mr. 'Who's-yer-daddy,' my 120 lb. magnificent retriever mix, had been my most loyal companion for twelve and a half glorious years, never wavering in his promise to love, honor and protect.

CHAPTER 9

One Hot Day

NAIVETÉ ASIDE, THIS WAS SHAMELESS...

There were hints, invariable slip-ups, and blatant displays. When my husband started losing weight and tanning to a deep bronze in the dead of winter, I was oblivious. When he asked me to shave his hairy back, I obliged. But when he started going to the driving range regularly, I suspected. He hated golf and often said he would rather go into the forest and poke sticks in his eyes.

In the summer of his self-improvement and new-found love of golf, my husband insisted that our family, including the two dogs, attend the law school's summer picnic, another event he had always hated. His insistence was oddly coupled with a request for the girls to be dolled up and the dogs to be bathed and brushed. So, with two darling daughters and two well-scrubbed retrievers, and one suspicious wife, we arrived at the sprawling park on a hot summer day. The two dogs jumped down from the Suburban, and my two dolls, in the awkward early-teen-stage of life, shyly stepped down onto the running board.

We were greeted immediately by Lola, one of the new law student assistants in Alan's office, whom he had been gushing about for several months. Furtive glances were exchanged between my red-faced professor and his freckled-faced twenty-six-year-old staffer. "I've heard so much about you girls; it's so nice to meet you in person. And this must be Spanky and Jack," She said enthusiastically.

She seems to know an awful lot about us...

"I hear you're a pretty good tennis player, but I bet I could kick your ass," she stated brashly.

Oh, my God, she didn't just say that. I'm the wife of a preeminent professor. "Well, probably so," I replied. "Nice to meet you, too."

The picnic was a basketful of evidence for the rest of the day as I observed the interaction between my husband and aggressive assistant. They wandered off at one point under the guise of shooting hoops on a distant court in the park. Running three-legged races and tossing water balloons with my daughters against the other families, I had held it together, but their giddiness with each other did not go unnoticed, even by my girls.

"Do you think Dad has a crush on Lola?" Megan innocently asked.

Ya think? I wanted to reply sarcastically. But I brushed it off and responded as a mature adult. "I think he's just trying to make the new assistant feel comfortable."

As the day painfully unfolded, and just as I was about to dig into my plate of ribs and potato salad, Lola scooted next to me on the bench.

"Wow," she said, "you must be hungry. I'm too tired to eat because I took the red-eye from Iowa to get back here in time for the picnic."

"What took you to Iowa?"

"A family reunion."

"Why on Earth would you leave a family reunion in Iowa and fly back for a picnic?"

She turned her pixie face towards me and just smiled. Nonchalantly, I put my plate on the ground for the dogs.

Suddenly, I had lost my appetite.

Chapter 10

Rock-Paper-Scissors

MOMENTS TURNED INTO YEARS...

There are moments etched into memory and... there are moments that turned into years...

Years of deceit and detachment...

He had emotionally checked out of our marriage long before Lola walked into his office and into his arms, and he knew it. Although I had checked out of our marriage long ago, I didn't know it.

Sometimes love is a decision and not a feeling. How did I know what constituted a good marriage or good love, for that matter, as my only reference had been this marriage and this man for thirty-four years? We shared a bed, two daughters (who were hard to come by), a menagerie of furry pets, a beach house and trips to Europe, Sun Valley, Hawaii, and Las Vegas. We were also connected by our similar politics which gave our relationship a base. I had a good life, or so I rationalized. He encouraged my tennis and my travel with girlfriends; I didn't have standing to be unhappy. We shared red wine, knock-down-drag-out competitive tennis, and rousing games of cards with our friends, but we failed because we lived life on the surface, never sharing our dreams, our desires, or our disappoint-ments—never building a foundation of shared values or common goals. Sadly, we were disconnected by our inability to share our feelings, so we co-existed. He bided his time, knowing why. I bided my time, not knowing why.

Rock, paper, scissors…

On paper, we were a perfect match: athletic, sports enthusiasts, college-educated professionals with common friends. He had already been teaching law, and I had been getting my MAT (and would be teaching the next fall) when friends introduced us in the spring of 1974. Love at first sight? Probably not, more like, 'Why not'? We were married six months after meeting each other and engaged before I had met his parents. Red flags had been flapping, but I chose to ignore them because I heard only wedding bells. Flags did not fit my narrative of "happily ever-after" and "until death do we part."

I have now come to the realization that we were not cut from the same cloth. I came from a farm family, a rural small town where marriages, for better or worse, endured. Though I came of age in the turbulent Sixties, traditional family values still triumphed. Feminism was not in our vocabulary and June Cleaver was our heroine. Up until my junior and senior years in high school, my life followed an almost idyllic path. We played cowboys and Indians with our Indian friends, floated homemade boats down the creek and played sandlot baseball where we worked our way up through the bases. We galloped horses bareback through the wheat stubble and gorged ourselves on fresh green peas, sitting in the field on a hot summer's night as the Big Dipper hovered above. Not all of us got a blue ribbon or came in first, but the town was our oyster and it protected its pearls.

Paper covers rock…

He, on the other hand, was raised on Queen Anne's Hill in Seattle by parents who owned a boarding house. He lived in an affluent neighborhood with a view of the iconic Space Needle. He lived among kids who had stay-at-home moms, so at times, he felt like he came from the wrong side of the tracks. His mom, a gentle and kind woman, taught middle school all day, cooked and cleaned for her boarders at night, and raised three kids. His dad, an egoist and pseudo-intellectual, was into conspiracy theories and the Kennedy assassination. In 1974, the year we were to be married, many young women had been murdered around Seattle, and like many residents in the area, his dad had become obsessed with those killings. (In 1979, Ted Bundy, a manipulative serial killer, would be found guilty of these murders, and ten years later, he was executed.) The first time I met Alan's dad, he spent the whole night lecturing us about his findings. Alan and I were already engaged, but I'm not sure his dad even caught my name.

Alan's household had not been a happy place. As a young boy, he escaped to a park where he would shoot baskets for hours all alone. He could never confront his father and resolve his conflicted feelings, bordering on hate, so he suffered hidden wounds and carried this carnage into our marriage. Unfortunately, Alan's father died young at age sixty-five, never stepping down from his high horse long enough to make amends. The son became the father.

Scissors cut paper...

We were married in Spokane at the Episcopal Church on a clear, sun-filled day. Our rehearsal got off to a rocky start when the Episcopalian Father reprimanded Alan for not knowing the Lord's Prayer. "Son, you need to learn this by tomorrow." After a wild reception overlooking the Spokane Falls, where our friends took advantage of an open bar, we came home to a tiny rental and started our life together.

We went through the normal motions of marriage: we worked and had sex, and I watched him gamble. I cooked dinners, cleaned the house, and watched him gamble. I taught seventh graders, did yard work, and watched him gamble. I had six miscarriages, went on trips with friends, and watched him gamble. I entertained family during the holidays, appeared with him in bankruptcy court, and watched him gamble. I had four more miscarriages, went to Las Vegas, and watched him gamble.

Rock, paper, scissors…

After my eleventh miscarriage, when he left me to be with the mother of his son and then returned two months later, we made a pact to never discuss this again. Case closed. But, that vow of silence hardened my heart and turned it to stone! Long before Lola, I was hanging on to the bare fabric of our life by a slender thread…

Rock smashes scissors.

CHAPTER 11

She Came Casually

WHO WAS THIS WOMAN, THIS AFFAIR?

She arrived casually one Sunday afternoon, tapping gently on our front door. Knowing she'd been introduced at a neighborhood party a few weeks before, we invited her in. She easily joined us on our green leather sofa, nestling in between us as the kick-off was about to begin. She was fun and entertaining; quite alluring, especially to him. We were in our first year of marriage, so I was more reserved, wary of this inexplicable intruder. She left quietly after the final whistle, thanking us for our hospitality, so why was I so uneasy?

Without an invite, she showed up again the next weekend. On Saturday, she was decked out in Oregon gear, the telltale lemon yellow and green of the Seventies. On Sunday, she came in Forty-Niner gear, ready to watch the NFL game of the week; coincidentally, she wanted the same teams to win as he did. *Was this a come-on? Did she find total agreement attractive?* As the weeks went by, she became a familiar fixture in our house during game days. They rooted for the same teams; no rivalries ever ensued between them. Sometimes, I rooted for a different team, especially for my Cougars. I was a true fan. They were fickle, depending on who was favored. How could they root for a team one week and then the next week, root against them?

I became concerned, but also conflicted. She was generous and open, charming, and inclusive. Bottom line: we had fun as a threesome.

Weeks turned into months; months turned into years. She was moody and at times manic, running hot and cold. She bought us TVs for every room, so they could watch multiple games throughout the season. She started coming over on Monday nights and then Thursday nights, too. Football surrounded us in every room and on every channel, and then basketball and baseball. They rigged up a TV in the bedroom, so it could bounce off of the closet mirrors. They could be in the family room watching one game while viewing a different game from the mirrors. My brain could not reverse the image from the mirror, which reflected backwards. If a score on the bedroom TV read 41-12, it really meant 21-14. No matter, they were delirious.

He mastered the remote, which was a marvel in itself because he knew nothing about technology. He counted on me to do every mechanical and electronic chore in our house. He never fixed one thing or used one tool, but she forced him to learn every detail of the remote, so they could watch numerous games at the flick of a button. He bragged that he never saw an advertisement and could keep track of about five games at once. Her beguiling charm hooked him into full submission; she became his meth, his drug of choice. I did not want to be friends anymore. I wanted her out of our house, but I could not budge her.

My wariness spawned confrontation and idle threats, so they went underground. Even though they snuck around, they left a trail of evidence. Shady local bookies, her sycophants, and offshore accounts needed to be contacted and fed. I found evidence of her under the bed and in the trunk of his car: secret codes in large money amounts were scribbled on his long, yellow legal pads. My idle threats went unheeded. He would never cut her loose, so I "went along to get along," ignoring my instincts and values.

When our daughters finally arrived, she lavished them with gifts. They did not know life without her. She was a generous relative, an eccentric aunt, always doling out money in hundred-dollar bills. She sent us all to Europe several times with her ample blessings. Hawaii every winter; Sun Valley every summer. *Designer jeans, Ugg boots, Urban Outfitter skirts, manicures, pedicures…would she ever stop? How could I send her out of my children's lives? Was this normal? Was this crazy? Was there a downside, a day of reckoning?* For sure, chaos swirled around us, but it was the only life we knew. We were held captive without really understanding how.

The one time we got a break from her was when he was asked to file a brief and present an academic perspective to the courts. This monumental task took months of working with his staff, and replaced the rewards 'she' provided. His unique perspective and hard work paid off because he was asked to present an oral argument of his brief to the Supreme Court, a rare occurrence, and we were so proud. He controlled his environment masterfully, garnishing the admiration and attention he craved. He sent 'her' packing because even bigger money was at stake, and he bet on his own abilities of persuasion, which fulfilled his high-risk desires. Only then did we get a reprieve and a glimpse of what it would be like without her.

Sports was not *Auntie's* only fascination, especially after the Indian casinos were built. Trips to our beach house included her. The girls and I did not see them much, for they became mad for Blackjack and Craps and made hit-and-run trips to the casinos, always bearing gifts upon their return. Intermixed with the trips to Indian casinos were trips to Las Vegas—her Mecca. She introduced us to the grandiose spectacle of Vegas, with all its glitter, and convinced him he was a VIP. He loved the seduction, the risk, and the attention.

With his VIP status, everything was comped. We feasted on lavish dinners at Caesar's Palace, the Venetian, New York New York, Paris, Bellagio's, the Monte Carlo, to name a few. She reserved the fanciest penthouse suites with sweeping vistas of the Vegas Strip. She lured us to the tables on the casino floor after we dropped our girls and suitcases in the suites. I rationalized that the fruit baskets, chocolates and luxurious surroundings of gold-piped pillows, scented soaps, and wide-screened TVs could sustain and entertain our girls, who were too young to be in the casino. Looking back, I realize I had succumbed to her to please him, and in the end, I satisfied no one.

Sometimes, however, she would present us with bundles of money, and we three girls would go on a wild shopping spree in the facsimile of the Roman Forum. Fountains with Roman gods and an ever-changing fake sky created a surreal ambiance as we strolled the outlandishly expensive stores and munched on Wolfgang Puck's designer food. As we sat eating our Caesar salads and Italian infused raviolis, the stars overhead twinkled in a pitch-black sky. By the time we were picking at our rum-soaked tiramisu, the sky glowed pink and orange, bringing forth a magnificent sunrise. As we were arising from our table after paying an exorbitant bill, huge marble statues sprang from the deafening white-water fountains where rhetoric of ancient Rome spewed forth. "Hail Caesar" boomed throughout the fake Forum as the sunset hovered above, giving rise to the moon. Such decadence.

She wreaked havoc on his sleep, so he turned to wine and Ambien. When we were home, he could pour himself into his bed and sedate his brain to slumber, but Vegas required more ammunition: he required four or five comped bottles of the finest red wine and a couple of Ambien in order to grab a few hours of sleep.

One night, I was surprised when the girls and I returned to our suite around midnight, and their dad was stark naked on top of his bed, snoring loudly. I managed to get him tucked away before I tiptoed across the art-deco hallway to join the girls in the second bedroom. Several hours later, the doorbell rang and rang and rang, waking me with a startle. Imagine my astonishment when I opened the door and he walked in without a stitch, still in the buck-naked stage. Apparently, he had been sleepwalking, and had even taken an elevator a couple of floors down. He vaguely remembered that people in the elevator were averting their eyes…ooh, what a late-night gross out, even for Vegas. How he managed not to be caught on video and arrested for indecent exposure spoke volumes about his Teflon character.

To be fair, memories were made—not all bad. Las Vegas entertainment is world class. We saw magic shows, Cirque du Soleil, Celine Dion, Bette Midler, Elvis impersonators, Garth Brooks and beyond, all the way to a Mike Tyson boxing match which was stopped in the first round. The entourages and sycophants, oftentimes one and the same, belied reality. We got caught in this fake reality because a bubble surrounded every VIP on the Strip, protecting them from seeing the underbelly of addiction that propped up this fantasy.

Bubbles eventually pop.

PART II

Chapter 12

Alone in the Village

THAT FALL DAY IN 1967, MY LIFE FATEFULLY CHANGED

Funny what one remembers on a day that happened over forty-five years ago. Vividly, I remember the lime green Bobbie Brooks wool skirt and matching vest I had been wearing. Three round gold buttons fastened the vest, and the pleated skirt hit above the knee. Fire-red penny loafers and knee-high stockings completed the outfit. The closet in the bedroom was ajar, revealing clothes and shoes haphazardly strewn inside. The bed was unmade.

I was sixteen going on seventeen that fall day in 1967, when my life fatefully changed. My athletic, aggressive boyfriend threw me down on his parents' bed and took away my virginity. For over forty years, I have blocked out this event, preferring, instead, to remember the idyllic childhood in my hometown...

I grew up a farmer's daughter in the Palouse region of Southeastern Washington. We were surrounded by fields of green that covered the rolling hills in the spring, and then the myriad shades of green would turn to golden wheat by summer. After harvest, the hills of the Palouse would look like giant sand dunes. My family farmed three thousand acres in the heart of the Palouse, bounded by the majestic Blue Mountains. The undulating hills of lush soil and moisture at the foot of the Cascade Range made the Palouse the most productive wheat-growing area in the U.S. My ancestors hit the jackpot when they settled in the region in 1865. Today, many ghost towns dot the landscape with abandoned barns and old grain silos, but small communities like mine still stand.

The small community where I grew up had a population less than a thousand and was a non-transient, close-knit town. The twenty-eight kids I started kindergarten with were the same as those I graduated with in 1969. Truly, this village raised us all.

In the fall, the town would gather for the football games, and in the winter, the gym would be full to the rafters for the boys' basketball games. Apart from boys' sports, our high school depended on active participation in order to have a band, a cheerleading squad, a drama department, and a pep team. I did it all. I was on top of the heap.

"We are the Grangers, the mighty, mighty Grangers," my four-girl cheerleading squad chanted and the crowd joined in as the team was driving down the field.

At half-time, the score was tied 14-14. My cheer squad and I were performing at half-time, but two of us were the lead trumpeters in the band, so we did our school's traditional highland dance and led the crowd in a response-chant: "Everywhere we go, people want to know who we are?"

We shook our pom poms and the crowd shouted back, "We are the Grangers, the mighty, mighty Grangers." I cartwheeled off the field and ran up into the stands to pound out the fight song as the team came back onto the field.

Our small group of five Thespians not only performed a play, but also wrote it, directed it, and starred in it. When we performed it in front of the whole student body, the kids hooted at our corny jokes, and we all felt like stars.

Earlier in the year, I had a conversation with the band director about marching in the Wheatland Parade as a majorette. "I love playing trumpet, but can I be the majorette instead for this parade?" I begged.

Mr. Jones sighed. He didn't have a choice; we needed a majorette. "Okay. But next time, you play trumpet and pass the baton to Deborah."

"Yes! You have a deal."

Nestled between Walla Walla, home of the famous Walla Walla sweet onion and the burgeoning wine country, and Pullman, home of my beloved Washington State University Cougars, sits Grangerville, my hometown. The solo yellow-blinking light directing traffic on Main Street today is the same light I remember from childhood, a symbol of a town where little has changed.

There were two competing grocery stores: Wade's Market and Tom's Market, one uptown and one downtown on Main. Our family was partial to Wade's Market because Wade himself delivered a box of groceries to Mom daily. All Mom did was contact our local operator who sat in a little booth on Main connecting people with black cables.

By three in the afternoon, Wade would come whistling through our back door, placing the box of groceries onto our washing machine. After swimming all day in the public pool when the temperatures rose into the 100's and the pavement sizzled under our feet, my friends and I would head to the downtown grocery and charge a raspberry or sometimes a strawberry Popsicle. Monthly, Mom would pay the bill.

Simple living built on trust made our community a golden place at a golden time.

Every business was named after its owner, and they were members of our community. Tim's Pharmacy, which had previously been

Gene's Pharmacy, also let us kids charge various sundries. The best part about Tim's was the adjoining soda fountain where greasy fries crackled in the deep fryer and chocolate donuts were made fresh daily. In the back was a pool room where old men in suspenders and bib-overalls lingered all day, chalking up their pool cues with blue chalk and challenging each other, "Hey, Earl, how'd you like my kick shot?" Lucky Strikes or hand-rolled cigarettes hung precariously from their lips as each took his turn punching the smooth balls across the green felt.

As eighth graders, my friends and I had a daily routine of slipping into our reserved booth where we snacked on the greasy fries heaped high on a white ceramic plate. We squirted ketchup all over the fries from a clear plastic bottle and sipped on our chocolate or lemon cokes. Often, we would top this caloric snack off with the mouth-watering chocolate donuts still warm from the deep fryer they had been plunged into before our arrival. Luckily, I was underweight for a young teen.

Next door to Tim's soda fountain sat Clyde's of Grangerville, where every fall Mom would haul us in the door to buy our tennis shoes for school. Clyde's was the only clothing store in town, and the only store with a display window. The display was a hodge-podge of farm tools with a bouquet of wheat in a bronze pot. Even though Clyde's of Grangerville is now defunct and lies empty, the display window remains a reminder of simpler times. Cobwebs branch out in many directions from one farm tool to the next, making a sad commentary on years gone by.

On the corner of that same block sat an imposing red brick building, home and office to Lou, the town's only doctor. Lou had cut off my warts and removed my tonsils. Later in his illustrious career, he became the county coroner, which suited him better. He had botched my tonsillectomy and several others.

After Lou removed my tonsils at the community hospital, I was rushed back a week later, bleeding internally. I had been swallowing blood all week, but as a scared six-year-old, I did not want my parents to know, fearing a return trip to the hospital. On a cold and icy December night, my parents discovered my weakened condition and blood-stained pajamas. They rushed me up to Lou's in the middle of the night. He met us there and looked more frightened than my parents or me.

I slipped in and out of consciousness on the twenty-mile drive to the hospital. I remember my mom cuddling me and soothing me as we made our way slowly along the icy country roads. She smoothed my sweaty hair from my face, whispering, "I'll be with you; I won't leave you."

I screamed and kicked as they rolled me towards surgery because I didn't want to go back into that cold sterile room where an ether mask filled with fumes would be plunged on my face.

"No eefer, no eefer!" I cried out. My parents had to pry my strong grip from my mom's soft cashmere sweater, so the nurses could go through the surgery doors.

"I wish you'd never born me," I screamed at my parents as the surgery doors closed.

On the return trip, the stitches didn't hold, and I had to go back to the hospital for a second surgery. Two weeks later, I went home to Grangerville, having had a brush with death. Upon learning that Lou did not correctly stitch up my throat, requiring that third surgery, my dad punched him in the nose. Poor Lou.

Right across from Lou's on Main was Leo's Shell service station, where my dad and all the other farmers would gather around five in the afternoon to catch up on farm talk and their golf swings, while passing around flasks of whiskey. Leo was the hardest working German in the town and my best friend Sarah's dad. He would whistle while he worked. He served up gas cheerily and changed tires effortlessly for all his community. On the weekends, he would sweep the street in front of his house and trim his blue spruce trees to perfection. Upon finishing his yard work, he would take Sarah and me for a drive in his old yellow pick-up, stopping first at his station, so we could each get a frosty-cold bottle of Squirt. My favorite destination was Steptoe Butte State Park where we had a bird's-eye view of the wondrous Palouse in all its splendor.

The only thing missing for a girl in my community in the late Sixties was competitive sports. Oh, we had a limited volleyball schedule where we played our rivals three miles away about four times, and we played another team where we had to serve over the water pipes in a very compact gym, but we never had much in comparison to the boys. The volleyball coach was Mrs. B, who had the biggest boobs pointing straight out, forming a perfect shelf for her oft-used whistle.

"The only two certain things in life are death and taxes," she would espouse on a daily basis. Mrs. B. disliked me, maybe even hated me, because I was cocky and competitive, a freshman who earned one of six coveted spots on the varsity squad.

We had a dirt track where the boys had meets and some training. As a freshman, I wanted to compete in the district track meet in the 220, so I approached the home economics teacher, who taught me proper table etiquette and how to make a dirndl skirt. She also served as the track coach, though she had no interest or athletic ability. I knew I'd find her after school in her home-economics room. I found her sitting at her sewing machine intensely working.

I gently tapped her on the shoulder to get her attention. "Miss Arbunkle, I don't mean to disturb you, but I want to run track. Could you help me train?" I asked.

She looked up from her sewing machine and hesitated. I thought she might give me some good pointers, but she went back to her sewing project. "Well, Margy, just go out there and run," she replied.

So, like Forrest Gump, I did. I made my way into the District finals of the 220 held in LaGrange, a huge school by comparison, eventually placing fourth out of a field of about thirty-two. I jumped the gun twice and had only one last chance to get out of the blocks, which, of course, were foreign to me. Of all the ribbons handed out that day, no one cherished a white ribbon more than I.

Miss Arbunkle was also responsible for the girls' sex education. The lesson was very short. She drew a picture of a penis on the chalkboard and warned, "Stay away from this." That was it.

Our competitive activities pitted girls against each other. Instead of fostering cooperation, we competed for the best boyfriend, Prom Queen, cheerleader, and girl of the month. I desperately wanted to get "Best Personality" like my sister had received her senior year, but I was tagged with the embarrassing title of "Best Athlete" for a girl my senior year. I immediately threw the trophy away. Even though I was an athlete, I had been programmed to think of that award as a slight. My, how times have changed!

The two-minute sex-education lesson ultimately failed me because that fateful day in November 1967, left me alone and pregnant.

CHAPTER 13

Denial

PREGNANT AND ALONE...

One month after skipping my period, I decided I needed to confide in Sarah. I remember my outfit from head to toe: a burgundy and white pin-striped dress with a button-down collar. I was shuffling amongst the late autumn leaves in my red-hot penny loafers when I disclosed my secret.

"Sarah, I think I'm pregnant," I blurted out, catching her completely by surprise.

"What? You sure?" she asked. "What are you gonna do?"

"Well," I began to tear-up, "I don't know for sure or what to do, but I skipped a period."

As we walked towards her house, we hatched a plan, so that my adoring and trusting mother would not find out. Why I thought this unplanned pregnancy could be kept a secret in my town where the status of each of its villagers was known, I have no recollection. But anyway, Sarah and I decided I should burn a month's worth of Kotex.

My mom was golfing that day, so I ran home with resolve. I grabbed the package of Kotex from the pink bathroom cabinet, and hurriedly dumped the package in the burning barrel, prominently placed in our front yard. Mrs. Bailey, my neighbor from across the street, who was approximately ancient and had babysat me on numerous occasions, could have seen my ritual burning from her kitchen sink window. And the Whitman's, from whom I borrowed many eggs and cups of sugar, could have seen my strange actions from their driveway. I didn't care. My mother was forty-five minutes away, probably finishing up at the 19th hole.

When I threw the Kotex into the barrel and struck the match, I felt relief, as though I was burning the secret and covering it with ash. Poof! Up in smoke went the evidence that I did or didn't have a period, however one looks at this plan. As the smoke rose higher, so did my spirits. But they would only prove to be the unrealistic hopes of a teenager—*a child with child.*

As the weeks went by, I knew I had to let my clueless, athletic boyfriend in on my secret. Even though I had begun to hate him, I stuck with him; I just kept pretending, just kept denying reality. Negative events are remembered, but traumatic events become blurred, so I honestly cannot remember how he reacted, or if he did react. What I do remember is…life went on just as if nothing had changed. I was a cheerleader, thespian, one of four honors English students, a speech contestant, a majorette, a trumpet player, a tomboy, a sister, a daughter, and three-months pregnant. Needless to say, I was in denial, unable to confront my trauma.

Every weekend, my boyfriend would excel on the basketball court while I cheered him on in my green and golden-yellow uniform, which hid my small bulge. After the game, we would sit out in front of his house and fight. I was like a dangerous wild animal, crying out in the darkness. I had no one to turn to for any sound advice. I felt trapped like a soldier in the trenches—stuck in *no-man's land*, mired in mud. In 1968, there was little a small-town girl with big ambitions could do. I just kept on denying my pregnancy.

One Sunday in the spring, he and I went for a drive on the back-country roads, winding through mixed green fields of young wheat and barley grass. A serene, pastoral drive I always enjoyed, however, I was as tightly wound as a cat ready to pounce, so I jumped from the car. I did not look before I leapt. He accidentally ran over my right ankle with his studded back tire, leaving stud scars on my foot as reminders of that day.

He hurriedly drove me to the community hospital where an emergency doctor set my leg in a plaster cast. Thank God my mom had a nightmare a few nights later and dreamt that my leg was not set correctly. She arose the next morning and drove me directly to an orthopedic specialist. I was rushed to surgery, and every toe ligament needed to be sewn in place because they were balled-up like little rubber bands. My leg had been set with at least a half-inch gap in my ankle bone, so the surgeon screwed a steel pin in my ankle, closing the gap.

In spite of being five months pregnant and sporting a cast on my leg, I cheered my boyfriend's team on to victory in the district playoffs. I loved being one of four varsity cheerleaders who could perform for the crowds. At that time, cheerleading was the closest I could come to participating in competitive sports.

Sometimes I wonder what my supportive townspeople thought when they saw me out there, casted and five months pregnant. *Did I have them fooled? Did my mom know? Was she denying it just like her daughter?*

By the sixth month there was no more denial. I was dressed in a green and white striped skirt and blouse when my mom walked in the front door as I was about ready to walk out.

"You could have gone so far," my mom said, holding back tears.

I burst into tears, unable to utter a word.

By the next day, Mom had purchased three outfits for me that would hide my pregnancy until the end of the school year. When I walked into my bedroom after school, lying on my bed were a yellow and blue shift with a matching coat, a red linen empire dress, and orange and hot-pink culottes. They were all keepers and actually allowed me to carry on.

My dad was unaware until my mom finally disclosed my secret. He adored me, but from that day forward, he would not speak to me or stay in the same room I occupied. I had become like a leper to him. If I walked into the living room, he walked out. If I walked into the kitchen, he walked out. The pain ran between us like a wave crashing down, tumbling our souls, but, today, it is a fading memory—a wave upon a distant shore.

Before that pain-filled year, there were special times with Dad that I still hold dear. He believed I was the best athlete put on this Earth, so he challenged my dates to broad jump against me on our linoleum floor.

"Margy can jump nine squares; I'd like to see you do that." As my dates and I were trying to get out the door, my dad was still challenging them to the next competition—a footrace.

When I was nine, my dad came through the door holding a black left-handed baseball mitt (we were both lefties) and proudly handed it to me. Every night after coming home from a long day of harvest, he would throw me high fly balls that I would chase down and catch in my new leather glove. I still have my black mitt and think fondly of those few summers.

One evening as Dad was winding up to play hard ball catch with me, the ball slipped out of his hand and beaned our basset hound, Cleo. For three weeks, Cleo's eyes were up in her head, but they slowly reappeared, just like the lines of cherries in a slot machine.

In the spring term, I took an early arrival chemistry class and, just as I was ready to walk into class, I looked down at my red empire dress. A wet ring had surrounded my left breast; frankly, I did not know what it was or what to do. I made an about-face at the doorway and ran to the bathroom. I didn't fully understand Avocado's number anyway. I know that is not the exact name for the all-important chemistry number, but in the scheme of life, who cares.

That fateful junior year, I landed in the State Speech Championship to give my district-winning persuasive speech about the first human heart transplant. More than flowers were popping out in the month of May, but my trusty yellow and blue dress served to hide the evidence of an impending baby. My best friend, who was competing in the "After Dinner" speech competition, accompanied me and my dress to Spokane, where we helped each other with our performances.

Persuading my audience to accept heart transplants as morally progressive was the thesis of my speech. Unfortunately, I had memorized it word for word. Halfway through, I forgot what came next and froze.

I looked helplessly at Sarah, and in front of the judges she replied, "Don't look at me, I don't know your speech."

Mortified, I quickly took my seat. There was no white ribbon in store for me that day. I should have stuck with running.

Late spring, the Chamber of Commerce selected me to be the representative at Girl's State that summer in Olympia, our capital. Girl's State was a big deal where select girls from around the state attended a week-long session to learn about the political process and our Constitution. I wanted to attend and felt honored to be chosen, but my mom squashed my unrealistic dream. "Margy, you can't go."

I watched my mom pickup our black phone to decline, saying: "Thanks, Bennett, but Margy's leg is so badly mangled she couldn't possibly get around the Capitol. We sadly must decline the honor."

At the time, the gracious way my mother got me out of this predicament seemed perfectly rational but, with hindsight, what were the townspeople who voted for me thinking and saying? They had just seen me leaping around in my cast at the district playoffs. To this day, no one in the town has said anything to me about the pregnancy. They protected me from the knowledge that they knew, and I am forever grateful.

My mom came through for me. As the school year ended, she began telling people that I was visiting relatives for the long hot summer. In reality, I was shipped off to Portland to the White Shield Home for unwed mothers.

Chapter 14

Closed In

SHIPPED OFF FOR THE LONG HOT SUMMER

Leaving my hometown with my secret intact provided a sense of welcome relief. I would be going to a place where nobody knew me, yet they would be in the same boat as me: up a creek without a paddle.

From the back seat of my uncle and aunt's Buick, I folded my hands over my trusty yellow and blue dress and observed the different surroundings as we climbed a long hill towards the White Shield Home in Portland. Stoically, I watched as the big city closed in around me. The trees that shaded the route prevented any view of the wider world, creating a sense of claustrophobia. I was used to the wide-open spaces of Eastern Washington where the patchwork quilt of mixed greens, bright yellow canola flowers, and golden wheat covered the land as far as the eye could see. Nothing looked familiar, and I felt afraid and alone.

As we got closer, I grabbed my matching coat like a cloak of secrecy. In silence, we drove into the circular driveway of the White Shield Home. I stepped out of the car, put on my coat, and watched them drive away.

As I walked through the door, bearing heavy luggage, my secret became a reality, and the White Shield Home became my sanctuary.

Visibly pregnant girls in a range of ages, some dressed in tailored maternity dresses and others dressed in stretched-out, threadbare muumuus, would become my summer friends.

A blonde, blue-eyed nineteen-year-old greeted me at the front desk. "Hi, Margy, I'm Jenny. I'll show you around and introduce you to everyone." She grabbed one of my bags and started up the stairs, "Follow me."

Over the next two months, Jenny and I became fast friends and shared many secrets. What a relief to have a confidante.

I was planning ahead to give my baby up for adoption. Jenny planned to keep her baby and never wavered, so I found myself alone in my decision. I felt constantly flummoxed, not understanding why someone would come hide away in a home for unwed mothers only to walk back into society with a baby in arms. Why did they bother to come here if adoption was not one of the considerations?

When I met with the adoption agency in the reception room at the home, I spoke firmly. "I want the parents of my baby to be athletic. I want it to feel like it belongs because I'm sure this baby will be filled with athletic genes." That's all my inexperienced, youthful mind could muster.

Even though I wasn't supposed to be enjoying myself at the White Shield Home, as if I were at a retreat, we girls bonded like a sorority. We would all sit around and tell our life stories. The only difference was our extended bellies. We had the same dreams and goals; the same compassion and conceits; the same yearnings and fears as any real sorority girl—we had just gotten ourselves trapped or fooled or preyed upon.

Every day, I climbed the steep stairs to the screened-in porch where a row of sewing machines awaited me. The other girls and I could order material and patterns and sew away all day. A turquoise coat and dress, a blue wool dress and a few cotton maternity dresses for my final month steadily took shape as I sewed day after day after day. We celebrated the Fourth of July with corn on the cob and barbecued chicken. We cried at the birth of a stillborn, and we celebrated the births of each and every one of our 'family.'

Water gushed from my body as I went into labor on a Friday afternoon. I was alone and confused. I did not know what to expect from the birth. Babies were just born at the small hospital that was connected to our dorm, and then the bewildered girl with her swaddled baby departed with her family. Home in Grangerville, busily keeping the secret intact, my family would never be coming for my baby and me.

The actual birth process is a blur; I don't remember any details, but I produced a most beautiful blue-eyed boy with thick black hair. He and I were the only ones in the hospital that night, so I wrapped my hand around his little fist and stared at him most of the night. *I can't let you go, sweet, little boy*, I thought, as I sat leaning into his bassinet.

"Mom, I'm not giving up my son. You can't make me." I screamed into the phone the following morning. "He has thick black hair like you, Mom. I already love him. I'm coming home with him and you can't stop me."

"No, I'm sorry, Margy, that is not an option." She paused. "Use your head."

"Mom, I know, I know," I cried. "I just can't…"

"Margy," Mom interrupted, "you must face reality. You can't bring a baby home. You have high school to finish and college to attend. You're too young and not ready to be a mother. Adoption is best for everyone. Calm down and think clearly. You'll not be coming home with a baby."

I hung up, put my head in my hands and sobbed.

My sister, who was visiting her Portland boyfriend, arrived at the White Shield Home the following afternoon. She came with a potted plant in hand as the family emissary, ready to mediate between my parents and me.

I was sitting up in my hospital bed and my stomach started doing flip-flops. She walked in and set the plant on the end table.

She tried to pretend everything was normal, but the whole scene was awkward. I began to cry.

"Do you want to see my baby?" I looked longingly at her through blood-shot eyes.

"Margy, I just can't do that, please don't ask me to do that. This is so hard."

My sister swallowed a lot of convention and shame in order to be there that day, so I couldn't ask her for anything more. Having her there to support me was enough.

Within two days my blue-eyed boy was whisked away by his adoptive parents. I never saw him again. Several days later, I walked out the door of the White Shield Home, back into my hometown, as if nothing had happened that long hot summer.

Chapter 15

Routine and Ritual

WHEAT HARVEST HELPED EASE ME
BACK INTO MY HOMETOWN

The wheat harvest between my freshman and sophomore year of college proved to be a quick one. We were harvesting the mountain ground on the top, so I had to make a long climb up the hill in compound gear. When I finally reached the top, I hurriedly pulled into the stubble, hoping to read a few pages of my romance novel before being signaled to load. While engrossed in my novel, I heard a crackling sound and started to smell smoke. I jumped out of the cab, looked underneath my truck, and saw flames licking the belly of the cab. Alarms went off in my head: "Margy, we can always get a new truck, so get the hell out of the field if there is ever a fire." I ran down the dirt road as fast as I could.

Boom! My truck exploded, throwing a huge cloud of smoke high into the air.

My dad was on another section of the farm, plowing under the stubble. With horror, he saw the ominous cloud. He frantically began driving up the hill. When he saw me, he jumped out of his pick-up and hugged me tightly for the first time since my return from Portland. He was a stoic man, who found it hard to show his emotions, but he was so relieved I was alive, he let his guard down and showed me how much he loved me, how precious I was to him. Tears streamed down his face, and I collapsed into his warm embrace. Suspended in time with fire all around us, there was finally forgiveness.

Nearby farmers began to arrive in their jerry-rigged fire pick-ups. Although the farmers feared fire, no one knew how to fight a real one. The scene was right out of a Keystone Cops movie. The men, who were spraying their fire hoses from the back of their pick-ups, went flying out, and pick-ups were going in all directions, swerving to miss crashing into one another. They were working to keep the fire out of the Saint Joe National Forest, which abutted the mountain ground. All night from my front yard, I gazed up into the sky and watched the mountain ranch burn. Flames licked the skyline like tongues of terror. The scene scorched my heart. Regret singed my inner being as my breath caught in my throat. Tears fell as the smoke rose into a gray cloud above the fields, obliterating the sight of a full harvest moon. Throughout the night, fire raced through 640 acres of mountain farmland, ending the wheat harvest for my family. *Sorry, Dad. One grief added on another.*

My charred truck was left in the field for a year, serving as a monument to all drivers. My dad changed the exhaust system on all his trucks, so the pipes ran vertically up the side of the trucks, instead of underneath, where a truck could become a torch after a long mountain climb.

Two years before, wheat harvest was in full swing when I returned from Portland, easing my transition back into the community. The thirteen-hour days from dawn to dusk hauling the thrashed grain from the field to the storage silos left me no time to dwell on the baby I had left behind. I loved the ritual of harvest and the routine it provided. I would stumble out of bed at 5:30 a.m., pull on my grubby cut-off jeans, throw on a cotton tee, grab my lunch made the night before and slide sleepily into the passenger seat of the pick-up to be driven to the harvest field where I took charge of my wheat truck.

The first day on the job after returning from Portland, my dad drove me to the field. He patted me kindly as I climbed in the pick-up, but he spoke no words. That was the best he could do, and I accepted his gesture. Those next three weeks, where I was in control of a six-wheeler, were a Godsend; just me and my truck and the routine of harvest.

Many of our fields were high altitude at the foot of the Blue Mountains, so I would have to put my truck in the lowest gear to climb the steep hills. Descending the hill with a loaded truck required the same gearing, allowing me to slowly creep down the mountain. When harvesting the mountain ground, my dad always gave us stern warnings about gearing, for a slip-up could cost us our lives. A two-ton truck fully loaded with grain could become a run-away-train if it slipped out of low gear. I can only imagine the worry my dad must have had for our safety, and yet, he let us be the master of our own truck.

I learned the art by riding along with my sister who drove before I was old enough. I was an apprentice for a year, which meant I learned the art of loading a truck, but I couldn't drive it out of the field. Every day, I loaded the truck, working in unison with the combine driver to get a perfect load. Dad cautioned, "Whatever you do, don't hit the header and knock us out of harvest." The header churned out front of the combine, cutting the stalks and throwing them into the thrasher. The header was considerably wider than the rest of the machine, so pulling alongside the combine always quickened my pulse.

When I received a wave to pull under the spout, I would pull my nose from my book, rev the engine and race out to the combine as quickly as possible. Then I would creep alongside, positioning myself under the chute, mindful of the header. My head became a swivel: looking back, looking front, looking back, looking front.

I used the header as my marker and maintained the same speed as the combine. When I was in ready-position, I would signal the combine driver to open the chute, and grain would come spilling out into the bed of my truck.

Loading became a precise art. I had to speed up, then slow down to layer the grain and not let it concentrate in the back or front of the bed. Sometimes, I achieved a masterpiece, like a Michelangelo, but sometimes, I failed and wheat would spill over the truck cab. Every bushel of wheat that didn't land in my truck bed was money in the dirt. Whenever my dad was driving the combine, he threw a fit if I failed. I let him down once and vowed to work hard to gain back his trust. Relieved to get a full load, I would carefully pull away from the combine and head for the open road.

We didn't have air-conditioned trucks when I drove, but we had our own unique system. When we loaded the truck, we rolled both windows up tightly to keep all the dust and chaff from coming into the cab, and when we pulled away, the first thing we did was roll down both windows, which produced natural air-conditioning. Out on the open road, wind swept through the cab and the sun bore down on my left arm, yielding the infamous farmer's tan—above the sleeve, my arm was white as snow; below, my arm was brown as burned butter.

The routine and ritual of harvest eased my grieving, but harvest ended. I had to face reality: my senior year with the same twenty-eight kids I had started Kindergarten with, and one of those had been my boyfriend. The unspoken words of my dad had made it clear: I was expected to avoid any contact with "that boy."

Chapter 16

Rush, Rules, and No Regrets

FINALLY, OFF TO COLLEGE; GOODBYE HOMETOWN

She sits with her back to me, cradling a stiff drink. She is outside on the patio, staring into space. I am in the kitchen staring at the empty whiskey bottle. *I have done this to her.* All I want to do is crawl upon her lap and be consoled, be reassured, but she is unreachable now.

Give it time, time heals all wounds. It has only been a week since I returned and, on this hot summer night, my mom needs to grieve. She will never see her first grandchild. This deep pain cannot be shared, so she, like me, must suffer alone. How sad that this proud mother and good daughter cannot talk about it, cannot help each other, cannot dry each other's tears.

My sister was not home. She was rush chairman for the Kappa Kappa Gamma Sorority and had returned early to WSU to prepare for the incoming freshmen. My baby brother, six years younger, whom I had dressed in pink tutus and cheered for from every bleacher, did not know. His friends affectionately called me 'Moose' because of my athletic prowess in their touch-football games where I would take all those six-year-olds out with one shove. Like a guardian at the gate, I had become his protector and would shield him from my shame.

As I sat in the bleachers my senior year, the double standard controlled my life. I was no longer a cheerleader, just a civilian fan, but the father of my baby was the star. Unfair? No, just the way it was. I set my sights on getting the *hell* out of Grangerville, believing that nobody but my family and best friend knew of my past transgression. Ironically, I internalized the blame and held the shame; not even for a fleeting moment did I look at it differently. Society had done a brilliant job instilling patriarchal values in me.

I did my best to avoid him—not easy in a high school with only two intersecting hallways and a graduating class of only twenty-eight. Luckily, I was in advanced classes, so I didn't have to see him there, but often I would pass him between classes, and he would grab my arm and try to talk with me. I only allowed him one conversation, and it ended when he pointed his finger and mouthed the words, "You gave away my son." With tears blurring my vision, I grabbed my books from the locker, slammed it shut and ran into my next class.

As Salutatorian, I was tagged to give the commencement speech because the Valedictorian had been too shy. Standing at the podium in my green cap and gown, I felt honored to thank my hometown on behalf of my class. With tears held in check, like a dam that holds back a river, I looked into the eyes of my parents, my neighbors, and my village, thanking them for all their support through my eighteen years. I moved the gold tassel from left to right and never looked back again.

Finally, the day arrived. I became a freshman at Washington State University, anxiously awaiting sorority rush, which was a week before classes began. We were assigned a dorm and a roommate in alphabetical order. My roommate was Carly Abernathy, a comely, thin blond from Kelso. I was Margy Adams, a perky brunette from Grangerville.

Nervous anticipation hung in the air as we greeted each other and the incoming dormmates. Though eager to make friends and connections, we were keenly aware that we were competitors for finite spots on our favored sorority roster.

Preparing ourselves for the grueling week of Rush tea parties, we hung our carefully selected wardrobes in the closet, lined up our shoes, and put brush curlers in our hair. Before Rush week, each of us presented our resumes and references, which were loaded with activities, good grades, and gushing compliments. Many of us had already chosen our preferred sorority because mothers or sisters or aunts had secured our spot through legacy. My mother and aunt were former Kappa Kappa Gammas, and my sister was a senior in the Kappa House at WSU. I was especially looking forward to the Kappa rush party, for I felt confident I would soon be wearing the gold fleur-de-lis pin, symbol of the Kappa Kappa Gammas.

In party-sized groups, we fanned out like peacocks with a leader and, for two days, attended sixteen rush parties. Each sorority had a theme, dressed alike, and sang us in and out, making awkward small talk in between. The Pi Phis were blond and flashy, the Alpha Chi Omegas were natural beauties, the Delta Gammas were fun-loving with a nautical theme, but all the others blurred together, except for my legacy, the Kappas. Their party was on my second day. I stood outside, taking in the brick mansion and manicured lawn before the doors swung open. My sister stood on the second stair of the highly polished staircase, singing in perfect harmony with the sisterhood. She winked and nodded; I felt loved, and this was soon to be my home.

After an exhausting two days, we were told bids would be handed out at 7 p.m. that night, so we needed to be in our rooms. I knew I would get invited back to the Kappa house, and I had legacy recommendations from former Delta Gammas and Thetas, so I wasn't worried. Many girls were sweating it, but Carly and I were having fun chatting about the Pi Phis and Kappas. "The bids are here, the bids are here," one of the girls shrieked. I was handed my packet, plopped down on my bed and opened it.

Gamma Phi Beta wanted me, Alpha Delta Pi wanted me, and Chi Omega wanted me. I couldn't even remember where those sororities were located, let alone recall their themes or matching outfits.

Just as I was turning my packet upside down, searching for the for-sure Kappa bid, a girl peeked her head into the room. "Margy, you have a phone call."

With concern, I made my way down the hallway to the one and only black wall phone. "Margy, I need to talk to you," my sister whispered into the phone. "It's against Panhellenic rules for me to contact a rushee, but I'm sneaking over after dark. I'll be out front. Try to be discreet."

The air was thick and damp, leaving the sky too heavy to show the moon as my sister shifted her little red Toyota into gear, and we slowly drove through the campus in mind-numbing silence. She wound her way into a park far away from civilization to a place where no eyes or ears could see or hear. She parked and cut the engine. And then she burst into tears.

Through gulping sobs, I learned I would not be wearing the stylized French lily on my chest. I was dropped from the Kappas because of the baby. Like Hester from the *Scarlet Letter*, I was an undesirable—an outcast—branded with an identity society had assigned to all unwed mothers. Though the sister-bond was stronger than the sisterhood, we were products of a rule-bound society and lacked the wisdom or courage to buck the system.

The fog rolled in, enveloping my sister and me in a surreal setting. She was tearfully apologizing, traumatized by the harsh judgement laid upon her baby sister by her beloved sorority and the Panhellenic board, the ruling body of all Greek sororities. She gulped, "The board ambushed me and brought me before them."

"What?" I interrupted. "I'm so sorry."

She took a deep breath and sighed, "One board member looked at me and asked, 'Where's your sister's baby?'" She pounded the steering wheel. "I didn't know what to say or do. It was horrible."

I could hardly talk and stared straight ahead into the dark night.

I felt guilty and ashamed that I had put my sister through hell, but I stoically came to terms with my predicament and shed no tears of my own. "Let's not tell Mom; it will kill her."

"Whad'ya gonna do?" my sister asked, "I can't talk to you until Rush is over. Oh, Margy, my heart hurts. I can't help you. Will you be alright?"

"Look, Sue, I have few choices, but I'll be alright. Three sororities must not know because they've invited me back, so I'll become a member of a different sorority. Now, let's get back before you get into trouble. It's not your fault."

Upon my return, I filled out my preference list, putting the three sororities in alphabetical order: Alpha Delta Pi, Chi Omega and Gamma Phi Beta. At the Alpha Delta Pi party the following day, I was surrounded by smiling young women who were genuinely pleased I'd chosen them as my first preference. The next day, I became an Alpha Delta Pi and never looked back.

When I returned home for the winter holidays, a banner hung crookedly from the back window of the red Chrysler. It read: *Proud Mom of an Alpha Delta Pi.*

It really doesn't matter what pin one puts on her chest, for it's just a false symbol and does not make the girl.

Chapter 17

The Cloak of Secrecy

TO TELL OR NOT TO TELL.

"I certainly hope you're going to get married soon," my dad interjected as we were discussing my future upon graduation from WSU.

"Well, Dad, that would be great if I had someone to marry," I replied.

We were sitting in the living room where he and I used to watch the *Gillette Friday Night Fights* together. I had come home for the summer with plans to move to Seattle in the fall. I know he had been proud of my accomplishments at WSU, where I was a Student Body Senator and tagged for Mortar Board, graduating with a 3.75 GPA, but all I remember from that discussion was my father's eagerness for me to marry.

Within six months of moving to Seattle, I met my husband. Six months later we were married. We appeared to be the perfect couple, but we were deeply wounded individuals who were adept at covering our wounds—he with bravado and me with compliance. *Did I rush in like a blind fool because my dad approved?*

In our first year of marriage, I attempted to tell him about my past. I remember as if it were yesterday: we were walking on the south end of the Aurora Bridge, close to Canlis, our favorite old-time restaurant in the Queen Anne District. We looked like a normal couple, with me in my celadon-colored pants suit, which was my 'going-away outfit', and him in a blue button-down shirt and a pair of khakis, but we had so many secrets that separated us that it didn't even feel like we were married.

I abruptly stopped at the foot of the bridge and tugged at Alan's sleeve, letting others pass by. He asked, "What's the matter? We're going to be late for our reservations."

I gingerly broached the secret I'd been keeping locked away; I just couldn't carry on any longer, so I began, "Alan, I want to share a major trauma in my life. I've wanted to do this for a long time, but have never felt an opening."

Once I began, the story spilled out of my mouth like water from a fractured pipe. When I was done, he looked me up and down.

"That explains why your body looks different." His lack of empathy felt like being impaled on a rusty blade. There was no compassion or curiosity. There was just the drip of silence. He opened the door at Canlis, and we walked in.

The chasms of silence, the blind forging ahead…*go through the motions, don't say a word.*

Thirty years later in counseling, desperately trying to save my marriage, I shared my hurt. He listened with a wooden face and had the same indifferent reaction as before.

July 19th, the birthdate of my son, always brings a day of reflection. I am reminded of the years of silence and secrecy.

For most of my life, the cloak of secrecy has been mine to wear and mine alone. I lived with shame and guilt for putting my family through all this anguish, and it never dawned on me that I was a victim myself. I know my mom went to her grave with much sadness, not only mourning her first grandchild, but grieving a loss of her daughter's innocence, a loss so profound she never discussed the secret for the rest of her life.

Before the last rites were offered, I was alone with Mom, running my fingers through her silvery hair. I know she heard my heartfelt good-bye because, before her final breath, she gently squeezed my hand.

Five years after my mom's death, I was driving my elderly dad to a medical appointment. He no longer had any quality to his life and could barely utter a sentence, but he still turned to me from his passenger seat, and with tears in his eyes, he clearly asked, "What about the baby?"

Taking me by total surprise, I gripped the wheel tighter and mumbled, "Oh, Dad, that's so far in the past. I'm sure he has had a nice life." I patted him on the shoulder and turned into the clinic.

His question came fully forty-five years after my son's birth. My dad, my dear demented dad, who had been diminished to a shadow of his former self, needed to know before he could let go. Two weeks later, he closed his eyes forever and went to be with Mom.

After my parents were gone, my sister became the new matriarch of the family and broke the wall of silence, laying waste to my guilt and shame. She gave me permission to forgive myself by giving what happened to me a name: date-rape. I had lived so long with my own guilt, not ever discussing my past that it was difficult to confront this truth. Now, we talk freely and openly; but we don't dwell—we just live.

Several years ago, my brother was taking my sister on a farm tour, showing her all the new land he had leased. With his new openness and clarity after a winning battle over alcoholism, he turned to her and asked, "Why didn't our family ever talk about Margy and the baby?"

When she returned from her visit, she relayed this unexpected revelation, and I decided it was time. I printed off my journal entries that dealt with my past, including a letter to him, and quickly sent them off before I could change my mind.

Three days later, I received his text: "Read your papers; disturbing, but my problem. Love you, Joe." We will never talk about this again, but he knows and has always known. It must have been confusing to him as an eleven-year-old boy.

The hardest conversation of all was with Megan. When she was a junior in college at Western Washington, my marriage was falling apart. I drove to Bellingham, hoping to salvage some semblance of family. I decided I needed to share my past with her, but it only served to burden her more. She was losing her dad to a woman closer to her age and her weak mom was talking about a baby she'd given up for adoption forty years before. She was sickened that her mom shouldered all the blame, but also, that her mom dumped this shocker onto her already sagging shoulders. Things went horribly awry that day, but I couldn't put the genie back in the bottle. *Timing is everything.*

We never talked about this again, but Megan never forgave me for sharing my past. Six years after that hurtful encounter, Megan gave birth to my grandson. He wielded a magic wand, melting our troubled past away, and for several years, we had superficial bliss. Everybody has a past, but, sadly, Megan could not shake the anger and forgive me, so for now, we are estranged.

There is a time to be born and a time to die. Of those, there is no choice, but in between, that is all there is, one choice after another. Sometimes we choose rationally, sometimes we choose irrationally. Sometimes we choose with cool dispassion, sometimes with heated emotion. Sometimes we find ourselves in a quandary—inert and perplexed.

Though no one can fully escape the unfinished business of the past, should it always be shared? My closest ally, my housemate, a piece of my soul, my daughter Paxton didn't know. But after forty-five years, was it necessary to tell her?

To my great detriment, I had kept my past in a locked box, sealed tightly in the recesses of my mind. I felt that telling her might overwhelm and burden her, as it had Megan years before. Paxton—my miracle—struggled, languishing in the hospital for nearly two years… battled for her life after many surgeries, many setbacks…struggled just to live. Over the past few years my quandary, a puzzle more difficult than solving a Rubik's cube, was whether to share my past.

We had shared everything else. We had sung country songs at the top of our lungs on many road trips. We had walked up and down the hills of Seattle over the years, mapping out our lives, making sense of the chaos of our old life. Perhaps, my sharing would be selfish and overindulgent. Sure, the past had power over me, and I lost valuable time living, but I had thrown off the binds of secrecy and made peace with my past, accepting how things were, so, I decided to stay mum.

Life is a mosaic of everything: shiny, joyous moments and cracked expectations. There are no clean edges.

PART III

Chapter 18

Groundhog's Day Redux

GETTING TO THE CRUX OF THE MATTER

A groundhog will hide in its hole afraid to confront the harsh winter, but in modern culture, Groundhog's Day has come to represent going through a phenomenon over and over again until one can spiritually transcend it. And so it goes…

In the winter of 2006, I emerged from my burrow and shed my cloak of denial. Gathering tidbits and shreds of indisputable evidence, I realized that Alan was cheating on me again, and it became clearer and clearer as the days went on. I had my suspicions about the law student, Lola, who had worked for him many summers before, and whom I had first met at the law school picnic when the girls were in their early teens. I assumed she had moved on after graduation and had taken her shameless flirtation with her, however, she had recently shown up at one of Alan's seminars and then at a symposium where he was the keynote speaker. I realized I had to confront him.

He walked out of the den where I had heard his hushed phone call. "Alan, who was that?" I asked in an accusatory manner.

He had become an adept liar and didn't flinch. "Oh, just a student who I allowed to contact me at home. She is struggling with my contract law class. Why?"

"Come on Alan, that was not a professorial tone." I answered, placing my hands on my hips. "Do you have contact with that Lola girl? Why was she at your seminar?" I had so many questions, but knew I would just get lies.

"Oh, Margy, lots of my ex-students come hear me speak, or come to my seminars to get their continuing legal education credits. Lola works for a firm in downtown Seattle; I run into her now and then. It's no big deal, so calm down." He walked into our bedroom and shut the door.

I had accepted the late-night excuses to grab a beer with his buddy, and I had acquiesced to his new interest in golf and the speaking engagements he had in New York, Phoenix and San Francisco that didn't include an invite. But, when Lola had shown up at recent events, my suspicions ran wild. However, the next morning after confronting Alan, I had carried on as if nothing had happened, handing him his newspaper and a hot cup of coffee.

The event that finally had me scurry out of my dark hole, ready to face the sunlight, could only be described as desperate, a stupid move on his part.

It was getting late and Alan wasn't home yet. "Hey, Hon, I'm going to stop off at Costco on my way home, sorry I'm running so late," he randomly rattled over the phone. "What do we need? Asparagus, apples, wine…I'll get it all, don't worry."

"I'm not worried," I replied. "You're the Costco man, that's your thing. Geez, you sure you want to go this late? It's almost seven."

"Yeah, I had a late meeting with some of my colleagues, sorry. See you when I see you. Bye."

As I placed the receiver back in the cradle, my wheels were spinning. *Liar, liar, liar.* Over the past several months, I had become a sleuth. I had gathered a slew of calls on his cell phone from the same number and had googled her (I discovered that she had worked with him on his *amicus brief,* the one he had presented before the Supreme Court of the United States). I secured her address in case I needed to do a drive-by.

When he arrived home around 8:30, he busied himself putting away the groceries. My eyes zoomed in on the Costco receipt where the exact time of purchase was stamped at the top. Not wanting to call attention to the telltale receipt taped on the side of one box, I helped put away the food and recycle the boxes. While his back was turned and his head was in the pantry, I grabbed the receipt and stuffed it in my pocket. It doesn't pay to be oblivious to details when having an affair. He had gone shopping for these groceries at eleven that morning.

"Good job, thanks for helping. I'm bushed, I'm going to bed," he murmured.

"Goodnight. I have a good book, so I won't be in yet."

"Enjoy."

After he went to our room, I pulled the crumpled receipt from my pocket, laid it on the kitchen counter and, with a big fat sharpie, circled the time. *No wonder the asparagus looks so limp.*

I went down the opposite hallway and climbed into my daughter's bed. Fortunately, she was away at college. I did have a good book but, that night all I could do was stare at the words on the page, garnering courage.

He appeared in my daughter's room, tightly clutching the receipt. His explanation was a convoluted lie, and we both knew it. It was nonsensical babble, like a baby's first words. How stupid did he think I was? At that moment, however, as he stood over me, making his case, my courage to confront him with all the evidence waned. I had a plan, though. I just needed to have access to his car where I knew his flip-phone was stored.

It was the Saturday before Christmas right after the Costco incident. He had been riding the life cycle, engrossed in several sports contests on TV, wildly flipping back and forth using his favorite weapon, the remote. "Mind if I use the Suburban to recycle all the cans and bottles?" I yelled over the deafening volume of the TV and whirring bike. "The containers don't fit in my Jeep."

Muting the volume, he asked, "What?"

I repeated, "Do you mind if I use the Suburban for the recycling? The containers don't fit in my Jeep."

"Oh, yeah, sure," he replied, as he unmuted and turned back to his game.

I hurriedly loaded the recycling bins into the Suburban and took off to the store. My heart and mind raced knowing I had possession of my own weapon—his cell, the smoking gun. I gripped the silver phone in my shaky hand and dialed the ubiquitous number.

"Hello, Sweetie." Her voice sounded soft and sexy.

I slammed the phone shut and knew I could turn my back no longer. Though I had been afraid of my own shadow, it was time for me to find the strength to climb out of my hole and confront the truth.

Barely able to breathe, geared into panic mode, I strode into the house and threw the phone at him, shouting her number.

"Oh, for Pete's sake, calm down. It's only an emotional affair... you know I'm monogamous, but she's...um, um...well, she's my best friend."

Really? Viagra in your briefcase? And what does that make me? The groundhog swiftly crawled back into its hole.

CHAPTER 19

Cement Heads

KARMA WALKED AWAY

Sometimes when we are brought to the ledge, we are afraid to jump.

Though I mustered enough courage to kick loose just a small rock from the rubble of the past to expose a crumbling façade, my husband and I agreed to wait until after the New Year to deal with his "emotional" affair. Holidays are exhausting and stressful in normal circumstances, and so we didn't want to drag our mess into the already stressful season. Besides, our girls deserved to have their traditions kept alive and their family kept intact.

That agreement, however, did not stop the movie playing in my mind. I found myself going back ten years when I first met Lola at the law school picnic, where my husband and she were unabashedly flirting, doing the dance, flaunting their feelings in front of my daughters and me. That Christmas season of discovery, I drifted back to the end of that endless day.

As dusk fell on that hot August day ten years ago, I found our old Golden Retriever, Jack, sprawled out on the ice that had been dumped on the ground, officially ending the picnic. Having had one too many plates of ribs, he was done, as was I. I found the rest of the crew throwing tennis balls for Spanky, our young retriever. I corralled and herded all of them into the Suburban.

As we backed out, the dogs were already settled and snoring, and Alan was grinning from ear to ear. "That was the best law school picnic we've ever been to."

"Dad, I thought you hated those picnics," Paxton attested.

"Yeah, Dad, what's the deal?" Megan questioned.

"Well, this year, it was just special," he murmured as he glanced longingly out the window before driving away.

After that glaring display of puppy love, I ignored the obvious signs, rationalizing that he couldn't possibly be interested in breaking up our family for someone young enough to be his daughter, so I carried on, blocking out any suspicions. Not realizing that the chaos of our life was a disguise and a distraction, I held tenaciously to what was familiar.

In the last years of our marriage, Alan showered our family with *stuff*. Each Christmas, I seemed to get more and more cashmere sweaters, so by the time he had one foot out the door, I had sweaters in every color. For each Mother's Day, he progressively gave me more and more hanging baskets. Our last May together, I finally put my foot down. "Alan, I don't need fourteen hanging baskets. It looks like a plant nursery. And besides, I'd rather use the money repairing the gutters, making them stable enough to hang the baskets." Only in hindsight did I realize that these gifts were a distraction.

He didn't only indulge us, he bought things for himself too. The capper was his insatiable appetite for ugly cement heads. One day he came through the door carrying a black horse's head that could have been a double in the bed of the Godfather. I thought it was a joke. Soon after the horse head, came a Buddha head. Living among falling down gutters, peeling paint, broken locks and askance shutters, I then endured fourteen multicolored flower baskets tenuously hung from the gutters, and a Buddha head and a sinister horse's head pretentiously displayed amid the chaos.

During the holiday season of my exposé, our mutual unhappiness sucked the joy out of our shared holiday rituals, so we clung to our traditions in mind-numbing fashion. I buried myself in holiday preparations, overdoing the cooking, shopping, and decorating. Meanwhile, Alan hid behind alcohol, food, and college bowl games. He maintained a semblance of normalcy for the girls, building his roaring fires and hosting my family to a Christmas Eve feast where we had our usual boisterous and competitive game of cards.

His gifts to me that Christmas were all black: a black cashmere sweater, a black purse, and a handsome black valise. The only colorful present was an ugly pair of extra-large, pink plaid flannel pajamas, not a good parting gift. But I was great at pretending. I didn't want to kill the moment or seem ungrateful, so I went to my default setting of passivity, closing out the year as a dormant volcano dressed in pink plaid.

Fast-forwarding through those tumultuous few years, I can now laugh about that manic Christmas—and still, I feel some deep sadness for our last time together when he took his remaining items from our house—his home for over thirty years.

We were standing outside our front door beside the pedestal where the Buddha head resided. "Do you think I could have the Buddha?" He asked politely.

"Yeah, sure, it's yours."

As he juggled the heavy cement head, he turned and said, "I wish I could've been a better man."

With Karma in-hand, he slowly walked away down our brick path.

CHAPTER 20

The Four Horsemen

WE WERE OFF AND RUNNING

Alan sat at the breakfast bar, sipping red wine, thumbing through John Gottman's *The Four Horsemen of the Apocalypse*, one of many couple's therapy books I had bought. "We're both in this book. I fit the behavior of stonewalling. You fit all the others."

"How many others?" I stood across from him at the kitchen sink, sipping my own glass of red wine. I felt my face flush as heat ran to my cheeks.

He set the book down and took a gulp of his wine. "Well, you probably fit all four, but definitely the first three. You're critical, full of contempt and, to top it off, you're defensive. No wonder I tune you out, which this guy calls stonewalling."

"I think you just described a vicious cycle. Listen to your attacks. *No wonder* I'm defensive!" I took several gulps of my wine as the words began to wound.

We lived in a chilly house without a warm regard for the other's feelings, countering with global attacks of "you never" and "you always." Our marriage of over thirty years was in deep trouble.

Dr. John Gottman uses the metaphor of the four horsemen to describe four behaviors which, when practiced regularly, predict the end of a relationship. He has named these behaviors: Criticism, Contempt, Defensiveness and Stonewalling.

Alan and I rode these horses hard and whipped them into a frenzy down the last stretch of our marriage. We had gone to great lengths to find an easy way out, building an elaborate paddock, full of inner sanctums where we lived our lives. We fed and watered the four horses equally, filling the stable full of wild thoroughbreds. Right alongside Alan's favorite horse, Stonewall, ran Obsessive Gambling and Serial Affairs. That trio stuck together in a tight pack, boxing out Honest Communication and Feel No Pain. Martyred Myself and Marriage Ideal ran after Security and Happiness, expecting they could be caught in the home stretch! But always, Defensiveness won the day, beating Suffer in Silence by a nose.

Both Alan and I rode tall in the saddles of our discontent, contributing to the marriage breakdown. I may have been critical and defensive, but his behavior with Lola clearly showed a deep contempt for our marriage, so this is my story, my race, and I will call it from my perspective.

When the holiday season ended and the New Year began, Alan and I found ourselves without any more excuses. We simply had to deal with our terminal unhappiness. He promised me that Lola was just an emotional affair, not sexual, and they agreed to stop meeting as "dear friends." I ran out to Borders and bought all the couple's therapy books, reading voraciously all day until he arrived home. Titles like *Should I go or Should I Stay* and *Make-up to Break-up* came with lists and exercises. I spent most of the day with my yellow marker, starring and circling the information that applied to us. When I finished, the books looked like the old Yellow Pages.

To my surprise, Alan suggested couple's counseling. In a million years, I wouldn't dream he would've been the one to take this approach. I stepped up, ready to confront our problems. I had believed Alan and I wanted the same outcome. I was tired of running from reality, tired of putting off the truth. Rationalizations and

"Yes, buts" were destroying us. When we found ourselves sitting on a couch with Nick, our therapist, Alan had a plan; I had hope.

When we first met Nick in his office, he stated, "Before you take a seat, I need a commitment from both of you to be honest in these sessions." He held out his long, bony hands and continued, "I can't help you if you don't tell the truth."

"Yes, of course, I understand," I said.

Alan nodded.

Nick's pinky finger pointed east at a ninety-degree angle from his middle joint and with that he gestured for us to take a seat, assuring us, "Anything you tell me stays in this room." He added with a chuckle, "It's an old basketball injury, comes in handy as a pointer."

His sincere regard for honesty and his self-deference made me feel comfortable and like we were in the right place.

He looked at each of us and began, "I ask for your commitment to saving the marriage."

"Saving the marriage is our goal," I restated, "That's why we're here."

Alan nodded.

Before we could get much further, I burst into tears and began to spill my guts about my teenage past. "I don't know where to begin," I sobbed. "I've got no one to share my bottled-up feelings with…I can't forgive myself for letting everyone in my family suffer. I feel so ashamed of being pregnant so young. Will I ever get over this?" I put my head in my hands and sobbed some more.

"That must feel like a really heavy burden. I'm here to listen. Maybe we can have a session just for you."

Nick's validation of my feelings felt like balm on a festering wound. "Really? Thanks. I'd like to do that. I need help."

Alan sat dispassionately, a stony, silent witness, with the same lack of empathy as the first time I had told him about this, thirty years earlier. I wanted Alan to feel my pain and to empathize. The first session ended with the distance between us feeling more, not less.

On our drive home after I had dominated that first session, I could not stop crying. I had shed my shield of protection—let down my guard—and Alan found a way to pierce my heart. "It's not always about you," he mocked.

I will never forget those words—they barreled over me like a tsunami wave and crushed my soul.

During the second session, Alan grabbed the reins and never let go. He reiterated that he wanted to commit to the marriage. "Yeah, I'm in, but…" he hemmed and hawed and began to wiggle his leg up and down.

I threw him a penetrating look. *More buts?*

His eyes darted back and forth like a hummingbird between two flowers. "Uh, uh…I think it would be a good idea to separate, so we can work on ourselves, rekindle our romance and reinvigorate our marriage."

That sounds so rehearsed, I thought, and I wanted to get up and leave but Nick interjected.

"How do you feel about that, Margy?"

I turned towards Alan and frowned. "I don't see how separating would help us work on our communication, and this is the first time you've mentioned the word separation." *Is this why he suggested counseling? Has he had this planned…Am I this stupid?*

The clock ticked, signaling the waning minutes of the session; it suspended us in uncomfortable silence. Alan scooted further from me on the beige couch, and I turned back towards Nick. "I guess it scares me." My mind was racing. I didn't know what to think. He said he was done with Lola—was this a ruse? "Um…um," I paused and took a deep breath. "Lola is supposed to be out of the picture and I just, I just don't know."

"I'm not seeing Lola," Alan hissed through gritted teeth. "This is for me, for us. We need to see…I need some space." He folded his arms in protest and sat back defiantly.

Nick glanced down at his notes and his pinky finger pointed at us, giving the illusion of lecturing. "Well, I've found in my practice that break-ups are dangerous for saving a marriage, but if you decide to do this, I have strict rules." He paused and scrutinized us, checking to see if we were paying attention. "Number one rule is no dating anyone else." He paused again to let that sink in and looked from one to the other to note our reactions. "Number two is for the two of you to date each other once a week and work on having fun, remembering what brought you together in the first place. We'll use counseling sessions once a week to work on your issues."

Alan had orchestrated a plan to separate—to break-up to make-up. He moved his chess pieces with mastery, assuring Nick and me that he would follow the rules and that Lola was out of the picture. Neither of us questioned his plan.

Like a prosecuting attorney, Alan made our lack of intimacy my problem, as if I were the defendant. On that day, in that makeshift courtroom, I had been found guilty and sentenced to separation. Regrettably, I accepted my punishment and vowed to do better.

After the second counseling session, Alan moved to a house in the University District, thirty minutes from our home. He did not want me to see it or help him move, claiming that we needed a *real* break-up—a split. He had leased a house until the end of April, setting a definite time period for our separation. The night before he left, my daughter and I made a bulletin board filled with family photos and all his beloved animals, with "I Love You" printed across the top.

As he walked away, bulletin board in hand, I had no idea how our story would end. I did not know how to live another way. A horse wearing blinders only sees the finish line.

Chapter 21

An Unrealized Bloom

OUR LAST CHANCE FOR HAPPINESS

In floral shops, the roses that won't open—called bullets—are discarded because they will never bloom. Unlike a rose bullet, "humans have the chance to bloom more than once—we can flower again once the pain of not flowering becomes greater than our fear." (Mark Nepo, Book of Awakening.)

For years, I lived like a discarded rose bullet—sowing the dormant seeds of habit—resigned to my life. I had lost sight of happiness and my responsibility to seek it. Happiness, like the fragrant rose, comes in many colors, but I had stopped growing, my roots had shriveled and my closed bud never bloomed.

In that first session with Nick, when I shared my hurt and shame of having a baby at seventeen, I wanted Alan to feel my pain and to empathize. Today, I realize, Alan had been incapable of extending himself into my pain, for he had left our marriage, emotionally, a long, long time before that counseling session.

Looking back now, I see that I had given him all the power—all the control. He had played both Nick and me as though we were pawns in a game of chess. I had lived in an internal world, unaware of what I could do that would matter from a man I made so unhappy. He would keep punishing me with silence and relentless slights.

Did I want to live in such a cold atmosphere?

I gave him a week to get settled in his house, and we agreed to wait until the second week of our separation before our first date. Due to all the stress and worry, I had been shedding weight for two months prior to our separation. I needed new clothes, so I used Alan's credit card and spent eight hundred dollars at J. Crew. In my brown linen capris and V-neck sweater, complete with new gold sandals, I was feeling like a new *sexy* woman. Despite all our animosity, I felt like a young schoolgirl as I drove to our meeting spot that Saturday night.

Alan had chosen a trendy restaurant in the University District, one he and his colleagues frequented after classes. We decided to meet at our athletic club, where I could park and jump in his car with him. I arrived first, so I could do last-minute repairs. I pulled down the visor, flipped up the mirror and applied my second layer of plum lipstick. I fluffed my brunette locks, took a deep breath, and climbed out of my safe haven. *A date with my husband of over thirty years…crazy.*

When we walked into the warmly lit restaurant, Alan seemed to be a familiar face. We sat in a booth and he was quick to introduce me to the waiter. "I would like you to meet my lovely wife, Margy." I was looking at the menu as Alan talked wines with his 'new friend,' the waiter.

"Might I suggest the basil-infused ravioli with the arugula and beet salad?" Raoul enthused.

"And which red would you suggest?" Alan inquired.

"The Walla Walla Vintner's Syrah would complement quite nicely."

"Okay, we'll have that, thank you, Raoul."

I felt like a small bird beating about the wires of a cage, but Alan spread his wings throughout the place, preening his feathers.

Pretentious came to mind, but I smiled and tried to strike up positive conversations. We talked about our girls and our dogs, especially our beloved retriever, Spanky.

"How's Da Man?" Alan asked, using Spanky's nickname.

As he drove me back to the club, my mind was reeling. *Is he going to kiss me?* He stopped behind my jeep, leaned over and kissed me on the cheek. "See you in counseling next Friday." He sped away before I even got to my car door.

The next week, my mom suddenly died, complicating Alan's plans. We never got a chance to bloom.

Chapter 22

The Last Day

HOW DO WE FACE A PARENT'S LAST DAY?

She wanted one last bridge game, but years before she had signed a Do Not Resuscitate order. No one in the family had expected a virus would take the life of my beloved mom in less than forty-eight hours, so she found herself all alone at the beginning of her last day on Earth. She had sent us home after visiting hours with the promise that she was feeling better.

When she was admitted to Walla Walla General Hospital the day before, she had a visit with my brother, her only son and youngest child. He still clings to the last words she ever spoke to him: "Don't mourn for me too long; I've had a long and wonderful life." Though her frail and bruised body had been ravaged by years and years of rheumatoid arthritis, she put up a daily fight to live life, never complaining of the constant pain in her gnarled joints. She was the proud, classy matriarch of the family. In his mind, our mom, who gave more than she ever took, was going to be around forever. He depended on her as the strongest woman in his life.

Death was not an option.

By the time my sister, the take-charge daughter, got word of our mom's looming failure, it was too late to get a flight home from

Hawaii. She had seen Mom the month before, so she had the vision of our sweet mother and their last hug, but a lingering sadness that she was not there to say her final goodbyes remains to this day. However, there persists a consoling fate that I, the middle-child, would get my chance to step up and be the strong one.

I had been playing tennis at my club when I received a phone call from my brother. "Hi, Margy. Don't want to worry you, but Mom is in the hospital. She'll probably be out in a few days. She was admitted last night, complaining of flu-like symptoms."

I pondered whether to drive from Seattle immediately or wait until I could be of more use when Mom returned to assisted living. Had it not been for my tennis friends, who insisted I go right away (because "You never know,"), I would have missed one of the most important days of my life. I would have missed the chance to support my mom through the end of her life—a key turning point in one's life.

I made it to the hospital just before the end of visiting hours. Mom, so shrunken and pale, was sitting in a chair, staring into space. "Mom, Mom, I'm here." I leaned down and hugged her thin shoulders. "You look good. Are you feeling better?" *When did she get so thin?* I thought as I released my long-held hug.

She looked at me through watery eyes. "Yes, I think so. Could you help me into bed? I'm so tired."

Lovingly, I scooped Mom into my arms and gently placed her into her hospital bed. Settling her in with a warm white blanket, I whispered, "I'll be back tomorrow and take you home to be with Dad." Before I left, my mom had already drifted off; the virus, which was stronger than its host, continued to rage a covert battle.

My brother and I stayed up late, rehashing life over several bottles of wine, assuring each other that Mom would come through and be there for the family like she always had. We both refused to accept the fact our mom had been failing for the last couple of years. We rationalized that she had to live, so she would. That's how we saw it—pure denial.

The phone call from the head doctor awoke us from uneasy slumber around 2:30 a.m., and shocked us with the directive to get to the hospital as quickly as possible. Mom had taken an irreversible turn; her kidneys had failed, and her body was shutting down one organ at a time. The last to go would be her heart. Panicked and speechless, we threw on our clothes, jumped in the pick-up and drove forty-five minutes, silently absorbed in our own thoughts.

Joe's not going to handle this well…I don't know what to say, I thought as we drove past family farms dotting the landscape along the familiar route from our farm to Walla Walla. Once on the ridge, we could see the hazy lights of the Walla Walla Valley. The wipers beat back and forth, back and forth, sweeping away a winter rain.

I sat staring out the passenger-side window, resting my chin in my palm. Tears, like raindrops, dripped down my cheeks. When I turned to look at my brother, his shoulders were heaving up and down as he held back his mournful cries. I reached out and placed my hand on his shoulder. "I'm sorry, Joe."

When we walked into Mom's room, reality hit…there was no more denial. Following the DNR but trying to buy time for our sister, the doctor had ordered a hard plastic mask placed over her face, fastened with a tight elastic band around her silver hair.

Whoosh. Whoosh. Whoosh. Air was shoved into her struggling lungs. *Whoosh. Whoosh. Whoosh.* Her eyes flickered around the room, anxious, yet resigned to her dire predicament. When she saw us, she tried to speak, but morphine had come on board, though not yet full strength. *Whoosh. Whoosh. Whoosh.* Buying time was hard work for everyone.

We'd never done death before.

I gently took my mom's hand and squeezed. "We're here, Mom, you're not alone now."

She held onto my grip and opened her eyes. She mouthed the words, "I love you." *Whoosh. Whoosh. Whoosh.* The hopeless situation almost brought me to my knees, but I stoically bent over and kissed her on her sunken cheek.

Whoosh. Whoosh. Whoosh…

"I'm bringing Dad here. I know he's eager to see you. We'll be back soon."

Whoosh. Whoosh. Whoosh…

My brother, unable to bear what was happening to our mom, stood frozen at her bedside, cracking his knuckles. "Nonna, I'm bringing Britney to see you. I need to go get her at her mom's." He ran from the room, visibly shaken.

Whoosh. Whoosh. Whoosh…

As I was leaving to get Dad, a nurse pulled me aside. "If that was my mother, I would remove her mask and load her with morphine, so she could die in comfort and peace."

Tearfully, I responded, "I hate that mask, I want to talk to my mom, but we're trying to get my sister here…"

"It's too late," the nurse replied. "You all need to let go."

"If we take the mask off, will she die immediately?" My heart leapt into my throat.

"There's no time-line at the end, everyone lets go when they're allowed to…"

"Do we need to tell her that it's okay to leave us?" *Is it okay?* I wondered, struggling with my own needs. *Could we do more? Could the doctors? Is it really over?*

"I'd tell her, but you know your mother, and you have to do what you feel is best for your family. If we take the mask off before her granddaughter gets here, there's a chance she'll die."

"My niece would be devastated, so I want the mask to stay on and the hourly morphine administered, so she can be somewhat cognizant. But after, I want to do as you have suggested. Can she still hear us when she's in a deep coma?"

"Hearing's the last sense to leave, so yes, say what you need to say, she'll hear you."

Accepting this stark reality, I expressed my gratitude. "Thanks for taking the time to tell me what to expect and how best to help my mom die." I hurried on my way to get Dad whose assisted living home abutted the hospital parking lot.

When I walked in, he was sleeping peacefully, and I almost lost the heart to wake him with the saddest news he would ever receive in his eighty-six years of life—the news that his beloved companion for nearly sixty years was going to leave him today. I sat beside him and rubbed his back. It was 6 a.m.

"Dad."

He awoke with a startle and looked at me intently. "Oh, Jesus Christ, it's time, isn't it?"

When we walked into the room, my niece, the youngest grandchild out of the eight, the "truest-believer" of the bunch, was telling her Nonna that she was going to a better place: "Nonna, you have worked so hard to be here for all of us, but you need to let go. I'm so happy for you that you're going to be with Jesus."

My brother watched from afar as his daughter said good-bye to his mom, a scene which he was totally unprepared to face. He had to get out of the room; he ran down the cold corridor of the hospital and fell sobbing to his knees. I know he wondered, as I did: *There has to be something the doctors can do to save her.*

My dad and I walked in as the good-byes were ending...

Whoosh. Whoosh. Whoosh...

The hugs and tears flowed all around.

I know my mom heard the whispers and the tears—she knew it was the end. Gasping for air through the hard plastic mask—*whoosh, whoosh, whoosh*—she screamed the words, "I love you, I love you," over and over again.

As planned, the nurse appeared and gently removed the mask. "We're going to give you comfort and serenity, Ma'am," she informed as she administered a maximum dose of morphine into the IV. Before long, Mom calmed her breathing and her restlessness subsided as she settled into her last living slumber.

"Ahhh, that doesn't look so bad," my dad intoned as he looked to me for affirmation. "Will it be long?"

"I don't know, Dad, let's go to the cafeteria and give Mom some rest. The doctors told us this would take hours. She's worked hard, let's let her sleep."

In the crowded hospital cafeteria, my dad regaled me with the memories they had had together. "Let's see, we went to Palm Desert every year for thirty-two years, lots of funny stories about golf and too many parties… oh, all fun. We played golf with ten couples for ten years…we called our group tournament the 'Sole Survivor' …I'll be the only sole survivor, now.

"I took your mother all over the country, let's see: Texas, New York, Charleston, Chicago…those were all bus tours…of course, your mom became best friends with everyone. I took her on several cruises from Alaska to the Mediterranean where she finally saw Europe…you know I was in Paris after WWII…I had chocolates, nylons and cigarettes…Ahhh, Paris, what a memory…"

He shrugged. "Well, anyway, your mother and I had a great life and she was a great wife. Everyone dies."

When my dad and I stood up to leave, a young man exclaimed, "Sir, I couldn't help overhearing. I'd say you had a fine life."

My dad turned to the young man and gruffly replied, "Don't get old." He walked out of the café with his head held high.

We started our vigil around 1 p.m. on the last day. Mom's kidneys had been shut down for hours and now her lungs and heart were working so hard to pump through the fluid building up in her body. A new sound had occurred, gurgling in every breath. She would eventually drown in her own fluids, and her heart would not be able to pump hard enough to prevent it. No one knew, not even the doctors or nurses, how long it would take, but she was deeply in a coma, and not feeling the effects of what we loved ones could barely endure.

All of a sudden, my brother jumped up and declared, "We have to do something. Can't we save her, please? There's gotta be a way."

"Joe, it's too late. I'm so sorry. Why don't you and Papa go back and take a nap. I'll call when it's getting closer."

My mom and I were alone, and it was time to say good-bye. The unvoiced pain we shared flowed between us like an electric current, "Mom, I love you more than my words can express." *Why do you have to die? I have so many more things to tell you.*

"You have been my rock, and I wouldn't have survived without you," I blubbered, now bathed in tears. "I'm so sorry to have put you through so much turmoil. I've truly learned what it's like to be selfless…you embody all that's good, all that's right." I stroked her sweaty brow. *God, this is hard. Why didn't I come visit more often or call? Mom, I didn't expect you to die, not now…I should've been here…* There is never a 'right' time to die.

"You don't have to worry about me any longer, Mom. I'll be fine and I'll look after Dad," I vowed. "Sue and I are so close and getting closer…she wants to be here in the worst way, but things have a way of working the way they should. I get to be the strong one. We three kids, we'll stay close like you've always asked us to do." *And we will, I promise.*

I bent closer to her ear, "Let go, Mom."

I know that she had many words to say; many last thoughts. I heard her speak within my mind: *Dearest Daughter, look how strong you are. You no longer have to stay in a marriage that is a sham. You're good and kind and capable. Dear God, I hope you figure this out and live the life of your choosing.*

Several hours went by where I watched Mom breathe in and out, in and out…in and out. She gurgled with every breath. Once in a while, she would raise her bony fingers to her neck and scratch. *Her life's been reduced to breathing in and breathing out.* I sat in the cold metal chair, staring at a shell of my mother, and taking my own deep breaths. *She had been such a vibrant woman…golf club champion several times…a selfless mother and wife…*

I placed a request for last rites, and then called Dad and Joe, "It's getting closer, you'd better come over."

I know my mom heard the Episcopalian Father saying a prayer. She heard the stifled crying. She heard us carrying our own grief like a personal piece of heavy luggage.

After the prayer, I'm sure she heard the sad pleas of her son, who had fallen to his knees beside her, pleading, "Mom, don't die, please, I beg of you. I need you. You are the only woman who ever loved me unconditionally. Please, please…"

Kerthump, kerthump…ker…thump…ker…..thum…p. I kissed Mom on her forehead, and carefully slid the two rings from her gnarled fingers. One, I placed on my own finger, the other, I put in safe-keeping for my sister.

As I stood looking out at the overflowing crowd at the Walla Walla Episcopal Church, I began the final eulogy: "The day my mom died my father proclaimed: 'Today, the world lost one of the finest human beings that has ever walked on God's green Earth…"

CHAPTER 23

Unbreakable Bond

HOW MANY BONDS WILL BE BROKEN?

In the beginning of one's life, there is, above all else, one mother. Mother and child form a bond, not from choice, but out of necessity. If one is so lucky, the bond becomes unbreakable like cement. Though there will be cracks, they will be patched or become a place where flowers grow…

When I received the call from my brother, who had tracked me down at my athletic club, I was unsure how to process his unexpected news. My brother, who never dreamed our mother would die, had played down her hospitalization. Before hanging up, he warned, "Dad has been trying to reach you. He's upset you haven't answered. He's standing beside me and wants to talk to you."

He handed the phone to Dad. "Where in the hell are you? Your mother needs you."

Instead of traversing across the state, I rushed south on I-5, connecting with I-84, the east-bound freeway that goes along the Columbia River on the Oregon side. As I drove east along the Columbia River

Gorge, I was preoccupied with my separation from Alan, and totally unaware this would be my last drive home to see my mom. Truly, this drive is one of the most scenic highways in the world—the white-capped waves of the Columbia River cut a deep swath through the red basalt cliffs on the dry eastern side of the Pacific Northwest, and the river eventually winds its expansive waters through the dense mountain forests resplendent with many white waterfalls that crash down from cliffs on the wet western side of the region. All that had gone unnoticed as I drove along the river on automatic pilot.

On that day, beauty escaped me because my thoughts were swimming in contradictions: the tangle of love and loathing that Alan stirred in me. As I was wading deeper into those thoughts, Tammy Wynette's signature song, *Stand by Your Man*, played on the radio. I turned it up and hung on every word, like an addict who clings to her drug.

My mom did not trust Alan ever since he had left me early in our marriage, returning two months later with barely an apology. *I've kept his indiscretions about his baby a secret, so might as well keep our separation a secret now*, I thought, as I turned north, heading for Walla Walla.

When I walked into her hospital room and saw her frail body slumped in a chair, I sensed the natural order of things had shifted. She was now like the child and I was like the mother. I realized I could not reverse it; I could not fix it, so I took on a new role: the strong, take-charge daughter.

After I realized how seriously ill my mom was, I called Alan. "Alan, my mom is in the hospital. Can you go home tonight to be with Paxton?"

His response was rather non-committal. "Oh, I'm sorry about your mom; hope she'll be okay. Gee, um… I'll go home if I can. Might be late, though. Paxton'll be fine."

"That's really not the point. I think she's concerned about my mom, and she worries about us. This is all new to her and Megan can't get home. Just get home, will you, please?"

"I'll try. Keep me posted about your mom, but don't call my cell. Call the office and leave a voicemail. I check that regularly; you know, I'm not very good about my cell phone."

When my mom took her last breath, I kissed her and slipped the two rings off her puffy fingers. That last breath. How can one explain it? One minute I had a mother, and the next minute, I only had her memory. A fundamental piece of me was gone forever when my mom passed away that evening.

My mom's sudden death complicated Alan's plans and limited his new "freedom." I called him shortly after she was pronounced dead. He didn't answer, so I left a message. I didn't want to tell Paxton over the phone that her beloved Nonna had died. I wanted him to tell her in person, to be there to give her a hug, to reassure her. It was bad enough that I had to call Megan and relay the news. Megan had been struggling with both Alan and me; she wanted little contact with us, but as a loving granddaughter, we had been communicating about Nonna.

"Paxton, it's Mom. Is your dad home?"

"No, Mom. He's at a fund-raising dinner and will be home later. Is Nonna doing okay?"

"Oh, Paxton, I...uh...uh...I'm so sorry, I don't want to tell you over the phone..."

"What, Mom. What are you going to tell me?" She burst into tears.

I didn't have to say anything else; Paxton knew. The contradictions of love and loathing had reappeared—I loved my daughter and loathed my husband. *Where in the hell was he? Did he have any compassion?*

I spent a restless night on the sofa in my dad's assisted living quarters, tossing and turning—adrift in my thoughts like a dinghy on a lonely sea—calling Paxton every thirty minutes, calling Megan, and then calling Alan. The swells of anger rose and fell like waves crashing through my mind.

"Paxton, is your dad home yet?"

"Mom, stop, I'm going crazy."

"Megan, have you reached Dad?"

"No, Mom, I'm sorry."

I sighed and dialed Alan again. "Alan, please pick up your phone. Call me. Where are you? You should be home with Paxton."

In the early morning after getting zero sleep, I got a call from Alan. "Margy, why didn't you call the office and leave a message like I told you?"

The juices of life boiled over as I paced the halls. I moderated my voice, trying to keep the lid on my anger. "That's what you have to say? I just lost my mother, and you weren't there for Paxton like I asked and you're lecturing me?"

"I'm home, now, Margy. I'll be staying here until you get home. What's the plan?"

"I'm picking my sister up at the airport, and we're going to make memorial arrangements. I'll be driving home with her this afternoon. We're thinking of having the service next Saturday."

"Look, Margy, I'm sorry. I would've come right home if you'd done what I asked. I didn't know. I had an obligatory dinner. I'll be here for all of you. See you later this evening."

He sat in the family pew, holding my hand. When I delivered the eulogy, a sixty-year love story between my mom and dad, what was Alan thinking or feeling? Was the sheen of tears a great charade? Or did he have deep regrets that we had no love story?

Evidently, our family togetherness and sharing stories of Nonna was too much for him because he had us drop him off at an Indian casino. "Pick me up in a couple of hours," he said; "You guys have lots of sharing to do."

"You're not serious, are you?"

"Sure, I am. Come on, Megan, pull in and drop me off," he slurred.

When I walked in to pick him up, he was at the cage, handing the cashier our joint Alaska credit card. He blushed when he saw me, putting his hand up to stop me from coming closer. I can't forgive or forget the night Alan maxed out the credit card on the night of my mom's memorial. For years, the dead-end path of resentment was easier than the road to forgiveness. But, perhaps it's time. "Forgive, but not forget?" "Forget, but not forgive?" Which is it?

My mom had never trusted him. She'd seen the cracks in his armor.

Mom, you would be so happy and proud of me, now. From the depths of my heart and soul, flowers in every hue grow, nourished by an unbreakable bond with you.

Chapter 24

Map of Life

WERE WE TRAVELING IN OPPOSITE DIRECTIONS?

Life is like a relief map, full of peaks and valleys with long stretches of mundane plains bumping up against rugged terrain. On that map, one also finds majestic rivers and oceans teeming with life, and hot, dry deserts thirsting for rain. When we are looking at the map from the right orientation, then we generally know where we are and where we want to go. If we're looking at it upside down or sideways, we will generally be lost…

I found myself lost and confused upon my return from my mom's memorial. My view of the map was small and sketchy, narrowing my views, and I didn't see many forks in the road. Alan and I weren't just looking at different maps, we were on different continents, but I couldn't see it. Though I thought we had been traveling in the same direction, he was going south, away from our marriage. I was living in a false reality.

Believing we were on the same journey, I asked him to move back home so we could work on our marriage on a daily basis. I felt as though the separation and the awkward, forced dates were a charade. Besides, I was grieving, and I wanted to have my husband comforting me. I needed him.

As I walked in the door of our house, having stayed a few extra days in Walla Walla with my sister, Alan was waiting for me in our rambling ranch kitchen with his bag sitting by his side. He had stayed through the weekend with our daughters, but it was clear he could hardly wait to get back to his "house of separation."

"Can we talk, Alan?" I sat down, facing him across our square oak table where we had sat with our daughters, sharing life and dinners for so many years. "I don't understand why you can't stay. We can still go to counseling and have date night, but this weekend thing is not working for me." Clearing my throat, I continued, "Besides, things have changed and you say you want to save our marriage, so I don't get it. Please stay."

He raised his eyebrows. "Do you want me to stay out of pity because you lost your mom? That won't work, Margy," he reasoned. "Look, I'm so sorry about your mom, but please, don't make me feel guilty." From his side of the square oak table, he scooted his chair back. "I'll be home on the weekends...we can play our tennis. I gotta go."

I had stopped listening. I was awash with fear and anxiety. Anger overtook me. I pushed the chair back from the table and ran out of the room, screaming, "Go, get out of here."

He jumped up, grabbed his bag, and walked out the door, yet again turning his back on his family.

Alan continued to lie his way through our counseling sessions, blaming me—and my past—for our inability to have a satisfying sex life. For decades, I had stitched old wounds closed, but they burst open in counseling, exposing a festering inability to forgive myself. I carried shame like a weight in the shafts of my bones, and he let me. He let me hold this guilt, always tilting the scales in his favor. The scars of my past became a roadmap to my soul, so I let him pile it on. I let him blame me. I had the freedom to stop being a victim of my past, a victim of his affairs, a victim of his control, but I chose to suffer in silence.

In attempting to avoid all my pain, I had lost my freedom. I was not powerless, but I chose to be so. I had the freedom to leave this gambling man, but I chose safety. I had the freedom to climb out of my dark canyon and pursue my own teaching career, but I chose a traditional path of stay-at-home mom. My map followed a straight route: out of touch with reality.

Our dates mostly consisted of rugged tennis matches followed by a barbeque at home. This suited me just fine as it was more realistic to our lives. I took up tennis in my thirties and found it became a passion. Alan encouraged this, which I always appreciated, and I became a skilled player. I could compete against Alan, who had been an all-star athlete, competing at the college level. Neither one of us gave an inch; neither wanted to lose. In hindsight, our tennis matches may have been the most realistic aspect of our marriage.

Three weeks after my mom's memorial, Alan had a symposium at Evergreen College in Olympia, so I decided to go to Walla Walla with my sister to visit my dad. We needed to wrap-up my mom's life. On our way back to Seattle, driving through the gorge along the Columbia River, my sister worked on my map orientation skills. "You know, Margy, you don't have to live this way." She had seen so much betrayal of my marriage, and she wanted me to wake up.

But I mused, "Oh, Sue, I don't think Alan could be married to anybody but me and *vice versa*." So much for my orientation!

When I walked in the door, the phone was ringing. It was Alan. "Hey, just wanted to say hi, and to give you a head's- up. The freeway is jammed, so I'm going to swing over to our beach place. The symposium was a great success, and I'm tired, so I'm going to spend the night, and play a few hands of cards at the casino. I'll be there for our tennis date, and look forward to filling you in on the symposium."

"Yeah, well, um, sure. Have fun, you've earned it. See you tomorrow."

I hung up with a lingering suspicion. I dialed his cell. "Hi, I do have one request."

"Yah, what?"

"What is the address of your house?"

There was an obvious pause. "Oh, Margy, why do you want that? You shouldn't see it. It's nothing to see…I just go to bed early, read my book…nothing to see."

"I want to see it. I want to see where my husband is living. I won't take no for an answer."

"Oh, for Chrissakes, whad'ya going to do?"

"It's a beautiful evening, and I'm going to drive over to that area and have dinner. So, what is it?"

My heart pounded and my mouth felt dry as I took a left turn onto the street where Alan had been living for two months. When I found it, all my suspicions were confirmed. The house was shrouded by overgrown shrubs and the grass had not been mowed. I made my way through the shrubbery up to the front porch and there sat an over-sized garbage can filled to the brim. The stench made me gag. Through teary eyes, I peeked through the front window. There on a Formica kitchen table sat the bulletin board my daughter and I had lovingly made for Alan. He had been there just long enough to drop it off.

Sadly, it was not even right side up…

We were, indeed, traveling in different directions.

Chapter 25

The Law of Probability

HAVE I LOST ALL MY MARBLES?

The Law of Probability states that the frequency of an event directly correlates to the likelihood the event will be observed. Decades ago, in my probability math class at Washington State University, we practiced event outcomes with black and white marbles. If there were more black marbles than white, the outcome of drawing a black marble was more likely.

The black marbles, evidence of Alan's cheating and dishonesty, were piling up. The white marbles, our chance at saving our marriage, were dwindling to zero. I was forced to deal with real life: the grey areas between what I believed and what Alan was really doing—— the grey areas between truth and lies.

Even though I had more proof than a bottle of Tequila Gold, I had clung to the few remaining white marbles, suspended in time by plausible deniability, unable to accept that Alan had been living with Lola for the last two months.

After driving away from Alan's 'rented' house with the overgrown image in my rear-view mirror, I knew what I must do: confront the truth. I had lived so long avoiding this moment that I really just wanted to drive away—drive away from my whole life. I felt like such a failure—he had just wiped his feet on my doormat for the last time but, still, I hesitated. *What am I going to tell my girls?* I asked myself as tears dripped down my cheeks. Spanky, my faithful companion, leaned over and licked my tears away.

I woke-up after a fitful night's sleep, put on my pink cashmere sweater and butt-hugging jeans. I dabbed on matching pink lipstick and glanced at myself in the mirror. For a fifty-six-year-old woman, I was looking pretty svelte and sexy.

"C'mon, boys," I called to my dogs, "Let's go for a drive." It was 7 a.m.

Though I had finally accepted that Alan had been living at Lola's, I still believed he had spent the night at our beach house and would be home, ready to play tennis later that morning. This ride with my two canine companions was just going to be a drive-by—an exploratory excursion.

A block from Lola's address, Spanky started to hoot and holler, rocking my sturdy jeep. He had spotted Alan's Suburban before I had—the law of probability was in play. I shook my head in disbelief as I pulled behind Alan's SUV. Surely, he couldn't have lied about everything. Surely, he had been alone at the symposium. Surely, he had been at our beach house, playing cards at the nearby casino. Surely, he wanted to save our marriage…he had said so in counseling. Surely, there were one or two white marbles left? Some hope, some element of truth somewhere?

Summoning all my courage, I took a deep breath, stepped out of the car, and walked numbly through Lola's unlocked front door.

Two panting dogs greeted me as I proceeded through the living room. Finding my way to a hallway that led to the bedroom, I was halted in my tracks by Lola, who stared, facing me in the doorway, hastily adjusting her robe. She ran by me, sobbing. I stepped into the bedroom and there stood Alan, stumbling by the bedside, trying to pull on his white briefs.

"Oh, God, Margy."

"How could you?" I screamed.

I ran into the kitchen where Lola was hunched over the counter, cradling her head in her hands. "How could you do this to me? How could you break up our marriage? You're a whore and a cunt." I had never used those words before; I didn't know they were in my arsenal.

Alan grabbed me and pulled me outside onto Lola's front yard. I fell to my knees and slammed my fist into the grass.

"How could you humiliate me, lie to me? You said you wanted to save our marriage, but you were living with her the whole time."

"Margy, stop! You'll wake the neighbors."

"I don't care! I don't care if I wake the whole neighborhood," I hollered loud enough to wake the residents along several blocks of colorful bungalows stretching along Lola's gentrified street.

Leaning down to me, he grabbed my arm and pleaded, "C'mon, please, let's get out of here. Get in my car."

I recoiled from his touch and screeched, "You're not coming back, get your *stuff*..."

He ran back in and came out with a sweater, a blanket, and a pillow. He was crazed, red-faced, and I knew he had left more behind than his clothes. He looked at me with round eyes. "Please, don't blame Lola. She's such a nice person. Please, leave her alone. Leave her out of this."

This was more than I could bear...my head was exploding. I snapped, "Oh, please, please spare me the lecture. She's a conniving bitch, a sl..."

"God, please stop screaming." His eyes grew even rounder. They reminded me of Spanky after he got caught eating out of the garbage can.

As we drove away in his Suburban, our dogs—who had witnessed this sordid scene—looked forlornly out my jeep window. We drove around in shock, staring straight ahead before he finally broke the ice. "What are we going to do?"

My arms shot out like a sarcastic question mark. "We? Whad'ya mean?" I hissed. "There is no *we*. What are *you* going to do?"

He slowly exhaled, "I want to come home…Gawd, I'm sorry. I'll get help getting over Lola; I want to stay married."

Yeah, sorry you got caught.

Through gritted teeth, I explained, "I can't have you in the house right now. I can't make a decision just like that."

"Please, let me come home," he murmured. "And for God's sake, don't contact Lola, leave her alone."

I smacked my palm on the console, swiveling my head sideways so I could fire from all cylinders. "What the fuck? Shut up about her. Just go home and get some stuff and get the hell to that awful leased house. Just quit being so pathetic. See you in counseling next week."

I jumped out of his car and slammed the door. Halfway to my car, I pivoted and ran back just as he was pulling away. "Stop!" I yelled. I banged on the window. "I need to know. How did you swing the house deal, and why did you bother?"

His face puckered. "Calm down. You're in a panic, I know, but look, Margy, I want to put this whole mess behind us. Will you let me prove myself?"

"Answer my question…the stinking house…"

"Crissakes, Margy, it doesn't matter now."

"To you, but it matters to me."

"Lola found it on Craig's List. She's really good with computers."

I bet she is.

The reality was harsh and the probability undeniable. I was no longer dealing with black and white marbles, but with love and lies…I could hear the crash of marbles and the shattering of glass, breaking through the grey areas of my life.

CHAPTER 26

Turn the Other Cheek

TIME TO PUT THE PAST IN PERSPECTIVE...

The stories of our lives carry pieces of truth and meaning over time. But it is the sweat and tears of telling that reveal greater truths, and the gift of time that puts them in perspective. It is the telling that heals...

Deep within me lie hidden chapters, and the telling is painful. How does one admit to being a doormat or the weighted clown who bounces back after being punched in the nose? In front of many car lots, a flailing Gumby is blown around, arms and legs all akimbo. Several years ago, as we were driving by a bright red Gumby, who was scraping and bowing, Paxton remarked, "Hey, Mom, that reminds me of you when you used to follow Dad's every command."

So this next chapter gives me pause, makes me ashamed of my malleability and my inability to stand-up for myself. How can I explain my extreme form of "turning the other cheek?" How many cheeks was I going to turn? How many insults was I going to accept? How many second chances was I going to give Alan?

After discovering Alan and Lola naked together in the bedroom of her house, I finally had the truth, but no resolve. I found myself alone, sitting on the beige couch across from Nick. I came with a sense of helplessness, unable to muster the courage to change things. I was still clinging to the "marriage is forever" ideal.

Trying to figure out a way to tell him why I was alone, I fidgeted and hemmed and hawed. *Why didn't I practice or think about what to say?* "Uh, well, it's a long story, Nick. Alan couldn't face you today, so I'm the designated partner. But he's promised to come next week alone. He wants to try, he does."

Nick nodded. He was well-trained in the art of letting his clients figure it out for themselves. I remained well-trained in the art of enabling, unable to see another way to live.

As the story unfolded, Nick didn't say a word, but nodded to let me know he was listening, while scribbling a few notes. When I finished, he shuffled through our file, locked his piercing brown eyes on my misty blue eyes and offered his perspective: "Affairs are exciting because they're risky, but ecstatic love that's characterized by sexual energy always passes. The bloom of romance always fades, and if the relationship was built on shaky moral ground to begin with, it's doomed to fail."

He continued with two pertinent questions. "How could Lola trust Alan? How could Alan love someone who was so willing to lie to his family?"

He tapped his pen on his desk. "Think about it, Margy."

For two months, Alan and I went for intensive counseling where we got away with using a broad brush to paint our lives with whitewash. We never confronted the issues that got us there in the first place. Nick had probably heard our story a thousand times. He looked at Alan intently and asked, "After all this, how could you and Lola trust each other going forward?"

Through clenched teeth, Alan answered, "Nick, I'm not seeing Lola; we're over…but I have to have closure, and I can't do it in a letter. I need to see her in person to end it for good and to get the rest of my stuff."

My mind was reeling but, of course, I acquiesced. My cheeks ached from clenched teeth and my heart raced, for I did not know how to negotiate my world—a world driven by fear.

Alan was finally living in his leased house because Lola and he had too much to lose, and he needed to convince me that Lola and he were done. He claimed that he had turned over a new leaf, but that he just needed one last dinner, one last night.

Alan was moving home on April 22, so he planned the 'last' dinner with Lola the night before he would be coming home to his family.

On April 21, I wrote him a letter. I had been filling my head with self-help and save- your-marriage books, so I believed that words would bring him back for good.

Dearest Hon,

I know you are facing a painful experience on Thursday; it is also painful for me for different reasons, but I am doing my best to understand the process. I cannot control how you feel, nor would I want to…I can only control how I respond, and I promise you I will give you time, patience, and honesty. I love you for just who you are. I have made a choice to fight for our marriage because I believe that we can achieve something that few partners ever achieve: a mature love, filled with joy and romance unfettered by unrealistic fantasies and expectations. I know that I am your best chance for a happy life; we have many compatibilities, plus the everyday things that matter so much: walks with Spanky and Tucker, our books, our philosophy, our tennis, dinners with our daughters, the comfort, and now the sex which has a chance to get better and better since we have freed ourselves of limiting expectations and are open to all the possibilities. I will add more because I want you to realize how full and complete our life can

be and really in lots of ways always has been: our friends, our
family, our sports (Huskies/Cougars), our future grandchildren,
my family, our "good history," a renewed sexual relationship,
admiration, and honest communication. I am looking forward
to the day when I am #1 in your mind…the day you see my
full worth and value…the day you want only me and will
fight for me as hard as I have fought for you. I feel secure in the
commitment you have made to the marriage; I hold on to that
and trust you will finally be home with us for good, and we can
walk into old age hand in hand without regret. I love you.

Your loving wife.

The next day, he came home, walked through the kitchen door and
stuck his head into the fridge, looking for a space for his boxed,
uneaten dinner. I heard him rumbling around, coughing, so I came
into the kitchen. He turned toward me and his flushed face gave me
my answer. He was on the verge of losing it. "Margy, you're going
to have to help me. I just said goodbye to my best friend." More
hurtful words could not have been spoken, but I hugged him and
mumbled something I felt he needed to hear.

That Saturday, having made arrangements with Lola to retrieve
his belongings, Alan moved his clothes and various sundries home
for good. I had no idea of the magnitude—in came the Tommy
Bahama shirt I had carefully picked out for Valentine's Day several
years before, the Bose Radio he had ordered, which I had forgotten
about, the blankets, the pillows, the laundered dress shirts—I held
back my tears.

I folded and hung all his clothes, neatly arranging them while he
sat on the deck, listening to a baseball game, and reading his book. *If I*
would just do more, he would love me more than Lola. He's home. I've won.

When I found this letter seven years later, on the other side of this heartbreak, I gagged because it was filled with psychobabble. I cried. With seven years of perspective, I now see with my eyes wide open. I was as big a liar as he. All those platitudes, all the whitewash. Today, I have found wisdom—I no longer live as an apology for who I am.

Looking at the letter one more time before putting it in my box of memories, I shook my head in disbelief and wondered how or why I could ever write that. Really, I was sweating because it was so pathetic. What book on relationships had I been reading? Jesus wanted us to turn the other cheek, but not grovel and become a whipping post.

Remember, I warned, the telling would be painful.

Chapter 27

The Sabbatical

COULD A BREAK FROM OUR LIFE SAVE US?

Before my separation from Alan and the discovery of his tumultuous affair with Lola, I knew about the sabbatical. The law school rotated the professors through a sabbatical cycle, giving them a term off, and it was Alan's turn to take three months from teaching. Sabbatical stems from the Latin root, Sabbath, and means a 'ceasing' or a rest. This sabbatical could not have come at a better time for us. In fact, it was our last chance to break from the vicious cycle our marriage had become.

Alan had three months off to do anything he wanted, and we had tentatively planned to travel throughout Southeast Asia, spending a week or so in Australia. One morning, while we were drinking our coffee and reading the newspaper, Alan surprised me with his change of plans. We were several months from July, the start of his sabbatical. We needed to cement the plans. "Margy, let's go to Australia for six weeks, and really explore one country, instead of hopping all over, spending time in airports. Will you pin down places to stay, at least for the first two weeks…then we can be spontaneous after that? We can use our air miles, so will you look into that, too?"

I smiled at him and nodded.

He continued, "I want to be home in the fall for the Huskie games. I won't return to work until October, so maybe we'll take a car trip, ending in Palo Alto where the Huskies play Stanford. I'll get us tickets and be in charge of the car trip, maybe go to Reno, first. See you tonight."

As he walked down our brick path, I peeked out the kitchen window, feeling a sense of relief and genuine happiness. I had never questioned Alan's motives for wanting to stay in our marriage, but maybe, just maybe, he had finally thrown in the towel, or, as his best friend advised: "When you run out of gas, you park the car at home."

As I sat finishing my last cup of coffee at our square oak table, I glanced around at our sprawling ranch kitchen. *Comfortable* came to mind. The years between us were accumulated everywhere, and it occurred to me that love and habit had blurred together to make a life. And, maybe, just maybe, Alan felt the same, resigned and resolved to move forward. *Could it be a true sabbatical where Alan would finally leave Lola behind? Would this trip revitalize and re-energize our marriage?* I jumped up from the table with a renewed spirit, ready to tackle life.

When we stepped out into the cloudless blue sky of Sydney, I had already adopted the oft-repeated slogan of the Australians: "No worries, mate." We flew seventeen straight hours to Sydney, and spent one night with plans to stay for a week at the end of our trip. I had planned the first few weeks around the tropical paradise of Queensland. It is the only place in the world where two World Heritage places come together—the 350-million-year-old Daintree Rainforest swoops down to the pristine white sandy beaches that touch the Great Barrier Reef.

The next morning, we boarded a small Qantas aircraft for a three-hour flight to Cairns, our first stop in the tropical wonderland.

We had packed light with summer clothing. It was the Australian winter but, to us, it was like our summers in Seattle. The summers in Queensland were rainy and unbearable, reaching temperatures of 120 degrees, but their winter months ranged in the 80's with relatively low humidity. We hit the proverbial jackpot, waking every day in paradise. We also left our cell phones and computers at home, bringing along the essentials: our tennis racquets and books aplenty.

We both had goals for this trip. Alan wanted to get into the best shape of his life, exercising every day. My goal, though unvoiced, was to reconnect with Alan, and I knew that tennis gave us our best chance.

Over the long seventeen-hour flight, we discussed the places we wanted to see and generally discussed a daily game plan. "Alan, I have an idea. Let's play tennis at every town and city we stay in."

"Great idea, hon! But you know I'm going to win every set."

"Not if I have anything to say about it!" The challenge was on. We duly recorded each set and game count in our travel book.

The tennis courts in Cairns were heavenly. We played four sets on grass. After four hard-fought sets: Alan-4; Me-0. Would he succeed?

One thing we quickly realized was the need for a car, so we rented it in Cairns with the agreement to return it to Sydney, six weeks later. As we headed for Port Douglas, driving on the wrong side of the road (at least to us who were used to being on the right side!), sweat trickled down our brows and the scent of molasses hung like thick syrup in the air. Riding along in this tropical land, surrounded by fields of sugar cane with stalks as high as Iowa corn, we settled in for a magical adventure. Alan smiled and remarked, "We're not in Kansas anymore, *Toto*."

In our two weeks at Port Douglas, we played thirty-seven sets of tennis on three different surfaces, morning, noon, and under the lights at night. We were steps from the tennis court in our family-run resort and a mile from the grass court complex. Pure joy…I won two sets, ending his dream.

We fell in love with every aspect of the area, including the famous Four-Mile beach, where the white sand stretched forever. The golf course we hiked around every morning posted signs on the water holes, warning: "Beware of Crocs." Being in a tropical paradise, away from our life, allowed us the freedom to forgive each other and the space to begin to heal, but we never mentioned our demons because we had so many distractions and adventures, we didn't have to face them. It was the perfect getaway.

We acclimated to the small-town feel and blended in as locals, shopping at the Saturday Market and going to the local coffee shops and cafes. I ate breakfast each morning at Soul and Pepper, an open-air café, while Alan lifted weights at the local club. Oftentimes, I shared my Portuguese sausage with a friendly bird, which would perch on the rim of my plate.

As we fell in love with Port Douglas, we also tried to fall in love with each other again. Did we succeed? We napped with benefits, renewing our physical intimacy, but then we would retreat to our books, which allowed us to go into our own world, so we never had to share our intimate thoughts. I reread *Thornbirds*, one of my favorite books of all time. I cried at Maggie's hard life in the Outback and mourned for the death of her son, Dane, and her unrequited love of the Cardinal. Instead of sharing my strong connection to Maggie with Alan, I kept 'her' to myself, always avoiding deep emotions. But we drank plenty of Australian Shiraz and had romantic dinners overlooking the yacht-lined harbor. We loved Port Douglas so much that we extended our stay, using it as a jumping off point to other surrounding sites.

We took the Poseidon cruise out to the edge of Australia where we snorkeled and acquired knowledge about the 1500 miles of the Great Barrier Reef. Snorkeling with scores of tourists was over-rated, however, as we were all whacking each other in the face with clumsy black flippers. I lost Alan in the churned-up water, but we had the same notion: return to the empty boat. We stretched out on the bench head-to-head and fell fast asleep…heaven. Upon our return trip, he and I went up front by the captain, and three whales escorted us into the harbor, entertaining us with cannon balls and vertical jumps, breaching high into the sky. Warmth flowed between us and memories were made.

We hiked the Mossman Gorge, but the highlight was taking a trek into the Noah Valley, a sacred Aboriginal part of the Daintree Rainforest, virtually untouched by man. Our guide looked and talked like Mel Gibson, "Hey, mates, before you enter this sacred place, you must first honor the Aboriginal ritual." He handed each one of us a piece of red ochre. Alan helped rub the chalky substance onto my cheeks, and we entered the dark, dank environs of the rainforest with red-streaked cheeks.

Our guide was an expert on the habitat for the rare species of plants and animals residing in the wet tropical rainforest, and he regaled us with strange names and stories that left a lasting impression. Trees with names like strangler fig and flying glass tree came alive as we walked by. One tree branch snagged my shirt, so I tugged to get it loose. Was this a metaphor of my life? The guide instructed, "That, there, 'ees' a one-way tree, mate, you can only get it loose one way like the spikes guardin' a parkin' strip."

As we approached the flying glass tree, it shimmered, and he warned, "Watch out, don't get too close, or it will throw shards of glass at you." Talk about survival of the fittest—the strangler fig does exactly that, strangles its host tree, so it can live. My favorite guide story was about the most poisonous snake in the world, slithering around in the rainforest. "If it bites you, mate, you won't even have time for a smoke. But no worries, they're very shy."

After leaving Port Douglas, we had four weeks to return our rental car two thousand miles south in Sydney. We gave up one day of tennis and drove up into the Atherton Highlands where we spent one night in a pastoral scene any artist would love.

We clicked off the kilometers, stopping for a night in Bowen and then Rockhampton. Both places were right out of the Sixties, which brought us back to our childhood. During our drive south, we chatted about the simpler times of our youth, and Alan was finally opening up about his difficult childhood. "Alan, look out!"

He slammed on the brakes, barely missing a kangaroo that had jumped out onto the road, "Phew, that was close." We managed to avoid further incidents, but it also ended the conversation.

We arrived in Bowen a few hours before sunset, so we decided to stop at the cement tennis courts in a public park and play a few sets before finding a motel for the night. The courts were rough and the nets were tattered, but Alan won the first set without giving me a game. I gave him a competitive second set, winning 4 games, however, Alan's game count kept mounting; he led 257 games to my 98. We found an inexpensive motel and a fish and chips hole-in-the wall to top off our stay in Bowen.

As grease slid down Alan's chin, he remarked, "Hey, mate, how about my win today?" I smiled, knowing that tennis really had been our elixir.

Though Rockhampton was smaller than Bowen, they took their tennis more seriously, and we found ourselves playing in a stadium-like setting. I dressed in all whites for our two sets on the finely finished hard courts, but it gave me no advantage. At the end of our stay in Rockhampton, Alan had amassed 263 games to my 103 games.

We headed south, through Brisbane where we had reservations for eight days on the Gold Coast in Noosa, another comparable area to Port Douglas. Noosa, like Port Douglas, had gleaming waterways, white-sandy beaches, and recreational opportunities beyond our dreams. We stayed in an apartment on the third floor above a tropical canopy. Every morning, we drank our coffee on the balcony where birds of every hue flew around chasing one another full of a cacophony that became familiar, and every night, we sat on our balcony, cocktails in hand, watching the fiery orange and pink clouds turn to smoky dark grey as the sun sank into the hinterland. As a west-coast, left-coast American, the sun rising from the ocean and setting in the hinterland baffled me.

Noosa's Gold Coast had a first-rate grass tennis club, where the members welcomed us with open arms. Alan loved hitting with the members, but we managed to play ten sets of competitive singles throughout the eight days. Though he won every set, I took him to a tie-break on the last set before heading to Sydney.

Though we managed to fit in four sets of tennis, our last week was spent exploring Sydney like tourists! Over the course of our six-week stay, we had both lost weight and gotten into shape, so we continued by walking all over Sydney. We wove in and out of the attractions around Darling Harbor, taking in Australian culture. We paused to listen to an Aborigine who was sitting on the pier, sending out haunting notes from his didgeridoo. We wandered into the aquarium full of Great Barrier Reef fish; trekked through the Botanical Gardens where bats hung from trees, looking like waxy black fruit; and finally, we meandered into the wild animal zoo replete with reptiles and animals found nowhere else on earth. We viewed a wandering wombat wobble into the wallaby's habitat to check out its food, and we ended the tour of Sydney's Wildlife World by glimpsing the shy, elusive Cassowary, listed in the Guinness Book as the most dangerous bird in the world. All these attractions were treats unto themselves. But, for me, the highlight was observing the many students taking advantage of all their city had to offer. At all the attractions, we saw kids dressed in their plaid skirts, silk ties, and embroidered emblem blazers—-no cell phones, no iPods, no laptops. Seeing high school and middle school kids jumping rope, wrestling, playing soccer or rugby, chasing tourist trains, and thoroughly enjoying life brought me back to my childhood and all its innocence.

Alan always prided himself on finding the best restaurants in the cities we visited, and Sydney was no exception. We strolled through a central park shaded by a mile-long canopy and ended up on restaurant row in a neighborhood called Darlinghurst. Our favorite was a family-run Italian restaurant where Alan was mistaken for Joe Namath on our first night. As we walked in, the owner greeted us,

"Mr. Joe Namath, welcome." Alan tried to explain, but the owner would have none of it. When we returned several nights later, the owner smiled, "Ah, Mr. Namath, come in, your table is ready."

On our last night in Sydney, we took the booze cruise where we circled the city, taking us under the High Bridge and out to the Sydney Opera House where the sunset bounced from the white sails. The city lights twinkled and the wine flowed. Alan snapped many pictures, capturing me holding a full glass of red wine in every frame. In the last picture, the sky had blackened, my glasses were off, and I was hanging onto the rail. But all good things must come to an end.

Alan seemed to lose his competitive drive on the tennis court where I won two sets quite easily, and though he won the last two sets, he didn't grab the travel book and record the scores as was customary; I did, instead, and added two exclamation points! By the end of our trip, we had played 59 sets of tennis; I won only four sets. He amassed 451 games to my 150 games. But, my plan was a success, and we learned that no matter the court, from cement to polished grass, the people and the love of tennis connected us.

On the morning of our departure, I became full of dread. I turned to Alan, who was nuzzling me in his arms as we slowly awakened. "I don't want to go home. I'm afraid." I rose up on my elbow and emphasized, "I don't want to lose you again. I want the magic to continue."

He reassured me with these words: "Don't worry, Hon, it'll be alright."

Chapter 28

Familiar Discontent and Demons

WILL THE DEMONS RETURN?

While on our six-week sabbatical trip to Australia, Alan seemed to rid himself of his two demons: gambling and Lola. Though unvoiced, he seemed to make a conscious effort; he tried to love me. I appreciated the effort and returned love in kind.

Maybe our marriage had never been based on love so much as knowledge, or time, or something impossible to kill—the cockroach of emotions. I knew all his annoying habits, and he knew mine. I lived alongside this person for over thirty years. We had created and experienced life together as one. He'd seen me at my highest point and my lowest, with all the imperfections. I was not myself, but half of a marriage. *How could I go on if he were gone? Can somebody be half of a person?*

That was my inexplicable state of mind upon our return from Australia. The reality of life did not go away just because we did. The familiar discontent began to grow before we touched down on the runway. The demons demanded attention. Though I opted not to know about one, I accepted and embraced the other. If gambling was the only salvo, the only 'demon' to take up space in his brain, so be it. "If you can't lick 'em, join 'em." Gambling was like spackle, filling the cracks and broken bits of our uneasy existence.

Our sabbatical continued with a trip via Walla Walla, through Reno, ending at our destination of Palo Alto where the Washington Huskies played a season opener against the Stanford Cardinal. Our daughter, Paxton, joined us for a week-long journey—a road trip.

One of the saddest stories of my journey pertains to the treatment of my dear, sweet dad, whom we visited for the first time since my mother had passed away, seven months before. My life at home in Seattle was in chaos right after my mom's death, and then I traveled for several months in Australia, so I did not visit my dad, leaving his care to my brother, who lived nearby. So, the fact that we were including a visit to Walla Walla thrilled me; I had been away far too long.

At the time, I had no idea I would see this visit as a sad story, but writing about it seven years later, made me ashamed of myself and my generation. I was trying so hard to please Alan and cater to his every whim that I did not see how we mistreated my dad.

We pulled up to Dad's assisted living apartment, and he met us in the hallway, which smelled like Pine Sol and too much potpourri. We had plans to play golf at the Walla Walla Country Club—his club and his treat.

I ran down the hall and hugged him. "It's so good to see you, Dad. I've missed you."

He was dressed in his Walla Walla Country Club polo, ready to go. "Come on, Dad, this'll be fun." He smiled. "Let's go. Alan is waiting in the car. Paxton is excited to see you."

Alan was antsy and rushed him, hurrying him on every shot. Alan was so impatient. But I did nothing because I didn't want to admit that anything was wrong; however, hindsight gives me fits. The man was eighty-six years of age and lonely.

At dinner that evening in the club dining room, Alan and my brother, who had joined us, carried on a sports conversation—the talk of two macho men. Setting his martini down, my dad looked at them through his thick glasses. "Talk to me. Don't I matter?"

Again, I did nothing but smile at him, amused how he still had three onions and no olives in his martini.

We were getting an early start in the morning, so we dropped Dad back at his place. "Paxton, you take Papa in, will you? Love, you, Dad."

Paxton held my dad's arm as they walked into his home. Looking back, I wonder why she was the only one who showed tenderness. What's wrong with me? I would like to have those precious moments back. Very painful memories, very painful. *Who were we, high and mighty on our sabbatical, who didn't have much time for a lonely old man?*

To this day, I beat myself up about how I treated my dad. He had been failing ever since my mom's death, and I soon realized that he was suffering through the early stages of dementia. Our treatment befuddled him: he was rushed through the golf course and ignored at dinner. Why didn't I do anything? Honestly, I don't know other than I didn't notice at the time nor appreciate the struggles of an old man. I was too caught-up in trying to please Alan and save our marriage (which seems inexcusable as I edit this story today).

After visiting my father, we headed to Reno. The drive from Walla Walla to the southeastern corner of Oregon is high desert and desolate. Much of the terrain looks like a moonscape. We drove for miles without seeing a car and had no cell coverage. As we crossed over the Oregon/Nevada state line, a small line of casinos stood before us like incongruous sentinels of the desert edge. When we walked into the dimly lit casino, the dealer jumped out of her chair and snubbed out her cigarette. The stained carpet crunched under our feet. Dust on all the trinkets, like gold slot-machine key chains, tickled our noses. Alan pivoted, gave a thumbs-down sign, and we walked back out into the scorching desert heat. We stretched our legs, grabbed an ice cream and off we drove.

We arrived in Reno, Nevada, that evening. Reno has an inferiority complex because it's not Las Vegas, so it tries hard. It really does. We were greeted by the famous sign: "Welcome to the Biggest Little City in the World." The gambling casinos, the restaurants and the shows were thriving. Alan was in heaven, gambling at the VIP tables for two solid nights. I could barely stand to watch his addictive personality reappear—the waste, the fervor. He fondled his tall stack of chips like a man with his new wife on their honeymoon. In order to sleep a few hours, Alan needed plenty of Ambien and plenty of alcohol. I stayed silent.

We drove west from Reno and arrived in Palo Alto before game time. I can't remember who won or if it was an exciting game. All I remember is how preoccupied I was with my thoughts. I didn't know then what I wanted, but the ache for something more was as palpable as a beating heart. I sat on the cold bleachers where I retreated to my inner sanctum. I felt time passing and life being postponed. *How had I let things get as bad as they'd gotten?*

I was still clinging hard to the notion that my life was like a well-worn cashmere sweater, soft and comfortable—that it fit me perfectly, and I didn't need to change. Jeez, I had a distinguished professor of law for a husband, two unique daughters, material comfort...*who am I to complain? So, he gambles too much?* Our house sat on an acre overlooking the Green River, and I played tennis at an exclusive club five times a week. I was loved by two dogs who thought I hung the moon, and three cats who couldn't care less. *Yes, I had a rainbow of cashmere sweaters and a pot of elusive gold waiting at the end, didn't I?*

We returned home, and Alan returned to teaching. I know the other demon showed up, but I ignored the tell-tale signs. The nagging suspicions, like an unraveling sweater, gnawed through my almost-perfect life. I felt overwhelmed, so I carried on as the dutiful wife.

In moments of intense disappointment and stress, we tend to experience the world in global terms. "Always. Never." But life is rarely about absolutes; it's usually about shades of grey...was that okay? *Was I okay being half of a person?*

Chapter 29

Stockholm Syndrome

A STORM WANTS TO MOVE ON...

In the fall of 2007, when the treetops burned with color, I felt burned out. I had spent the year in 'flight or fight' mode. From the death of my mom to the discovery of my husband's affair, I was exhausted and resigned. I didn't want to question my life anymore, so I found myself alone on Nick's couch giving him glowing reports about the sabbatical and the vast improvement in our marriage.

It would be my final visit.

"Can you believe that Alan is back home, Lola is out of the picture for good, and our trip was like a honeymoon? We have come so far that we don't even need to see you anymore."

Nick paused and he clasped his hands together, the pinky finger still pointing east. "Well, some couples are fast learners." He stuttered, seemingly at a loss for words. "Uh, uh...good luck."

A week later, Nick died from a massive heart attack while playing basketball, keeling over on the hardwoods after a drive to the basket. He was forty-nine.

So, what made me sit and lie to him on my last and final visit? With seven years of hindsight where I can finally see the 'forest through the trees,' I have some clarity, some explanations which point to human nature. I may be far afield, and I may be searching for answers where there are none, but at least I'm trying.

I agree with Mark Nepo that by nature, humans are awash in ambivalence, swept along by the fickle and skittish winds of life. Most of us don't want confrontation. Many of us are frozen by fear, choosing, instead, to have an unexamined life. Even though we know where deep things live, most of us drift along on the surface, hoping to avoid what lurks below. We compartmentalize our pain and shove the hurts into the recesses of our brain. "Honesty is the net by which we fish the deep," according to Nepo, but only seasoned fishermen choose to grab hold because they have nothing to lose.

The fallen leaves—yellow, red, and gold—swirled around my feet as I walked up the street to the neighborhood restaurant where Alan and I were meeting for our anniversary dinner. He had called earlier in the day. "Hey, Hon, can we do dinner another night? Uh…"

I sighed. "Alan, it's our thirty-third anniversary."

"Oh, God, I'm sorry, I can…okay, yeah, I'll be there. But can we meet there? I'm running late."

Just as I opened the door to the small bistro where we had celebrated many occasions, Alan came up behind me, holding a bouquet of flowers. He handed me the cellophane-wrapped mishmash of forced blooms with a spray of fake gold leaves—the kind of bouquet one hurriedly pulls out of the grocery store black buckets. Not wanting to seem ungrateful, I forced a smile. "Gee, thanks."

As we settled into our familiar corner booth, the annoying, pretentious waiter sauntered over to our table. "Good evening, Sir. Lovely to see you tonight." The white linen tablecloths, the black leather seats and the single red rose that graced our table were subtle *chic*, but he was a snob in search of a big tip.

Alan always took the bait. "Ivan, what's your suggestion for wine tonight?"

"Ah, Sir, what is the occasion? What brings you two beautiful people in tonight? May I suggest the Malbec?" Two words always came to mind when he was our waiter: brown and nose.

"The Missus and I are celebrating our anniversary. The Malbec would be perfect." Just for the record, I always hated being called the Missus.

After the wine was served, and we were just the two of us, alone, without pretension, I was hoping to recapture the magic that had overtaken us in Australia. Alan leaned in, took a sip of his wine and as if trying to convince himself, he said, "You're such a good person. You're so kind."

Huh, that's it? After thirty-three years of marriage, that's it? I was waiting for the "but", but it never came. We ate in awkward silence.

That was my last anniversary meal.

The leaves turned to brown mush and clogged the grates as the November storms moved through. We spent most weekends at our beach house, gambling up a storm. He increased his bets to astronomical proportions, but I sat there in compliance, wincing with each loss. It was as if I had Stockholm syndrome where I cooperated with my 'captor,' never questioning his actions. His values became my values, and I irrationally defended his gambling.

"Mom," Paxton begged, "you don't have to go with him. What are you doing?"

I turned and shook my finger at her. "Your dad works hard. He can spend his money however he wants, and sometimes you have to compromise in marriage."

She looked at me with disgust and stomped away.

As I look back now, one night looms above all others. We were at our familiar casino close to our beach house at Ocean Shores where Alan was their VIP. I was in my familiar seat, watching Alan risk hundreds of dollars at the blackjack table. That night I pleaded with Alan to let me take some chips and cash them in because he had won a boatload, and I didn't want him to give it all back. He shoved some black chips into my hands, and I went to the cage. Usually, they would count out the hundreds to me without question, but this time, the woman called the manager, and they huddled together.

"We can't give you the money without you signing this form."

"What form? Why?"

"Ma'am, we have to comply with federal regulations. You must sign that you're not laundering money through this casino." Being the good little captive, I signed, collected the bills, and went back to the table, slowly doling back to him as needed.

The trees stood as bare sentinels, casting short shadows over the wintry landscape as Christmas approached. Though the rains had moved on, other storms were rolling in, gathering on the home front.

Chapter 30

The Pause Button

'TWAS THE SEASON OF MY DISCONTENT...

When the days darkened early and the nights were long, I was trapped, trying to hang on to something already lost. I needed to hit the pause button—put life on the shelf and look at it. But it's not like that, is it? Life goes on regardless.

I had to keep talking to the people in my life, feed the cats, feed the dogs, cook the dinners, wash the clothes, walk the dogs, load the dishwasher, take a shower, fill the gas tank...

And then, Christmas was upon us.

I had to shop, shop, shop; then also trim the tree, decorate inside and out, wrap packages, write my annual Christmas letter, go to parties, drink lots of red wine, make fudge and homemade almond Roca, frost cookies, entertain family and friends...

Like a clock, I found no pause; I had to put myself on automatic pilot and pretend.

〜

Several hours before our close friends were to arrive for a card party, Alan's phone rang. He flipped it open and abruptly closed it.

I knew what that meant and confronted Alan, "Why can't you just be honest, Alan?"

"'Whad'ya mean?" he mumbled.

"You and Lola are seeing each other again. Can't you just admit that you…"

He turned beet-red. "Hon, we really are just friends. Really. We both like football and we just, um, talk and share about the Huskies and Iowa football. Honestly."

I stood in front of my closet, trying to find something to wear. I shoved one hanger after another. "Oh, please, why can't you let me go with dignity? Why do you torture yourself? Why?"

He came from behind and put his arms on my shaking shoulders. "Look, I'm conflicted." He tried to turn me around and make eye contact. "Can we get through another Christmas? Lola and I are just friends, really…I can't lose my family."

I rebuffed his attempt to hug me and slid my head into my shirt. Pulling on pants, I twisted the knife with his own words: "You always say that it's all about me, but really, Alan, it's never about me. Listen to yourself. Seriously, I don't matter." At that moment, Megan walked into the room and the conversation ended in awkward silence. Even though it felt like we needed that twisted knife to cut the tension in the air, we all pretended it wasn't there.

Our friends walked in and soon we were sitting around our square oak table where we four had logged many hours playing cards. Our game of choice was East Coast Pitch, a bidding and trump game. One of the rules of the game was that we each had a 'handle' instead of our real name. Our handle hinted at our personalities— Alan's was 'El Champione,' Bryce's was the 'Manager,' Christina's was 'Miss Christina' and mine was the 'Razor' because I was always on edge and feisty.

"What's your bid, Razor?" the Manager asked.

Alan turned to Bryce with a sheepish grin. "She's no longer the Razor. We decided she should have a softer, gentler name, didn't we, Hon?"

I nodded with a smirk. "Yeah, I'm now 'Ducky.'"

"Why? You're the Razor to me," The Manager intoned in his deep baritone voice.

I organized my hand of cards. "Well, everything is just *ducky*, so my bid is three spades."

In an attempt to be more desirable or more deserving, I complied with Alan's wish to change my handle. Why I didn't tell him to shove Ducky up his tailpipe, I can't really explain. I was wasting life abiding. Why? That is the question. I didn't feel appreciated, comfortable, or respected, but I stayed. Why couldn't I leave? Why couldn't I find the door? My chronic inability to change—to see the truth—kept me painted in a dark, excruciating corner.

Hell, I didn't need a pause button—I needed a panic button. All the trapped emotions burst on my thoughts like a thunderclap during the last Christmas of my marriage. Anger crumbled into loneliness, tears rolled into laughter and the cool face of indifference refused to acknowledge the pain.

As the night progressed, I cooked the dinner while the others visited in front of a football game. From the freezer, I grabbed a huge bag of Costco peas, which were in one frozen lump. Needing only a few cups, I started pounding the bag of peas on the tile floor.

Paxton walked in the kitchen door just as I had lifted the bag high above my head. She gasped. "Mom, whad'ya doin'?"

I gave her a smarmy smile and swung the bag to the floor. "I'm getting unstuck, I mean, the peas unstuck."

My daughter gave me a quizzical look. "Kinda harsh, isn't it?"

Like releasing steam from a pressure cooker, I raised the bag above my head and gave it another *whack* on the tile floor.

Paxton and I now refer to that 'release' as the 'Pea Incident,' and we laugh.

Life goes on regardless…take down the tree, pack the decorations, put away the china, throw out the uneaten fudge, drink the red wine, take

back the unwanted, ill-fitting gifts...feed the cats, feed the dogs, cook the dinners, wash the clothes, take a shower, fill the gas tank...

There is no pause button, only rewind.

PART IV

CHAPTER 31

New Year - A Beginning and an End

WAS THERE HOPE FOR A FRESH START?

The New Year is steeped in optimism. It is a fresh start, a ray of hope. Our resolutions abound with pledges to do better in all aspects of our lives. I have always loved the idea of a beginning and an end, the cyclical nature of a year.

But the last January of my marriage found me without a renewed spirit, without an end in sight.

I was cursed to keep old wounds alive, unable to slough off the past. Unable to forgive myself, I accepted three decades of bad behavior. I martyred myself. I transformed myself to Alan's ideal—anything to avoid confronting my own personal darkness.

I carried my troubles into the New Year like oversized bags, unaware how to lighten the load. I kept plugging away at life, taking refuge in unreflective pursuits without considering a different path. Like an anorexic, I did not know I was starving—starving for truth and authenticity. It was my fault, every bit as his. Yes, he was a 'bad actor,' but I suppressed the waves of hatred, passively accepting, and thus enabling the situation. I did not have the courage to tear down my self-protective pride and surrender.

I hid in the open, covering my wounds with layers of shame.

Three scenes—one each decade—have played over and over in my mind: three chances to change course; three chances to choose an exit ramp:

The girls were barely out of diapers when Alan decided to ride his bike three thousand miles across the USA one summer with his great pals, the Benson boys. As aging athletes approaching their mid-life, they decided this would be an important notch on their belt of life-time experiences. They put their back tires in the Pacific Ocean as they started their trek, planning to average a hundred miles a day. They hoped to put their front tires in the Atlantic Ocean in Virginia Beach thirty days later.

I had settled into a routine and was enjoying being a single mom for a month—enjoying the serenity away from the chaos that swirled around our family when my husband was present.

I had been sweeping my kitchen floor when a lady with official-looking material, a stern-looking smile and a black polyester dress appeared at my door. It was a hot summer day, and I had an open-door policy, so she stepped across the threshold when I greeted her, informing me she was from the IRS. I invited her to sit at the square oak table, the treasure from my grandparents' old farmhouse.

Putting the broom away, I joined her, not having any idea why she was there. She did not waste any time and started rambling off an unfathomable state of tax malfeasance, spreading forms all over the table. She moved her eyes around the big ranch kitchen and gazed out the sliding glass door towards the Green River and the silhouette of Mount Rainier. She started expounding on the possibility of a second mortgage on "my charming house" in order to pay off the back taxes, ten years in arrears.

She stopped short. "You have no idea what I'm talking about, do you? You're not aware of any of this, are you?"

I gulped. "Ah, no." She left shortly after my tearful reply, leaving a mound of information and directives stacked haphazardly on the square oak table.

That evening Alan called from his motel, as he did every night, filling me in on all the adventures experienced that day. After I finished with my tearful diatribe, his response bewildered me more than the taxwoman's. "You can get a divorce if you'd like."

Two young daughters, a husband somewhere in Kansas, a ten-year tax bill and that's my option?

This happened in the late Eighties, but I ended up staying another twenty years. I could have taken the other fork in the road, but, alas, I did not.

In the early Nineties, Alan informed me I was to show up in court with him the next day for a bankruptcy hearing. Having grown up in a farm family where we lived conservatively within our means, I was caught completely by surprise. I had no understanding of bankruptcy. It was an alien idea—and a shameful one.

"You'll have to give them all your credit cards. And tell the judge you want to keep things like your china."

I jerked my head out of my book. "A judge? How embarrassing."

We rode the elevator up to the courtroom in silence. I was so nervous to be the 'co-defendant' in a case where I was completely innocent. I barely remember the judge's questions directed at me, but it has left an indelible scar, and though the memory of the hearing has faded, the feeling of shame still remains. One statement Alan made to the judge, however, sits vividly in my mind. He promised the judge the gambling that got *us* into bankruptcy was under control and from a distant past.

I sat there and said nothing.

Alan turned to me one evening in early November of 2001, and nonchalantly said, "You have to drive me to the beach tomorrow. I have to appear in court."

"Okay, but why do I need to drive you?"

"Uh, about three months ago I got a DUI in Ocean Shores and spent the night in jail. I have to surrender my license and be processed." He coughed and slumped down in his recliner. "I need to warn you that they'll handcuff me to take me into the courthouse."

"Why wouldn't you have told me? God, Alan, what a thing to spring on me."

"I'm sorry." He paused. "It was horrible spending the night in jail..."

Does he think that makes me more sympathetic? I thought as I stared in disgust. *Like a self-centered child, it's all about him.*

His DUI and ensuing process did not affect him nearly as much as his innocent daughter, who paid a far greater price. She was only fifteen years old with a learner's permit, but he leaned on her to drive him to work in the rainy, snowy months of November, December, and January. Her private high school was in the city, close to the law school, so it made sense, and yet, she was an inexperienced driver and had to cater to his needs.

"Mom, who is Mark Gianni?" she asked me one morning at breakfast, while her dad was in the shower.

I spread my English muffin with peanut butter and took a bite, chewing on her question at the same time. "I think he's a gambling friend. Why'd you ask?"

"Because Dad calls him every morning and every afternoon and places bets with him." She took a bite of her muffin, hesitating to add, "It makes me uncomfortable."

My hushed tone now became a crescendo. "Oh, that pisses me off, Paxton. I don't know what to say except..."

She put her hand up to quiet me. "It's okay, Mom. I can handle it." She leaned across the square oak table. "One more thing, though. He had me drive him to a Western Union yesterday. What's that? He was all secretive about it."

What kind of mother allows her daughter to be an unwitting partic-
ipant in this inappropriate behavior? Again, I chose inaction.

It is often said: "No pain, no gain." When we confront and work
through our pain, we grow, but wishing for a different outcome will
never change the ending. Finally, I realize that there will never be
a fresh start or a new beginning without pain. Tragedy stays alive
by feeling what's been done to us, while peace comes alive when
we realize there will always be pain: *feel it and use it to come out of*
the darkness—just like a spring that bursts up higher for having been
pressed down for so long.

CHAPTER 32

Crazy

I DIDN'T THINK THE OFFICER WOULD UNDERSTAND...

"Paxton, Paxton, I need to talk to you, so sit down." I was flushed and my heart raced. This would be the last day of my marriage. I knew in my gut that the charade was over.

She plopped down on the leather couch as I stood pacing. "What, Mom, what is it?"

"Well, it's Easter, but your dad left at 11:00 this morning." I paused, letting that sink in. "Said he wanted to get to the beach to play a few cards and be rested for tomorrow's conference at Ocean Shores." I put my hands on my hips, stopped pacing and leaned down, so I was face to face with Paxton. *Poor daughter with a crazy mom.* "Why, on a holiday, did he leave so early? Hmmmm?"

She looked up, rubbing her thumb and forefinger together, a mannerism she uses when stressed. "That's just Dad; he gets antsy."

I threw my arms out with upturned palms. "Paxton, let's get real. I could no sooner go to PF Chang's and a movie—as he suggested when he threw me that hundred-dollar bill—than fly. I'm going to the beach and confront him. His gambling—well, really, his whole life—is out of control, and I need to deal with it."

She began to shake her head. "Okay, but maybe you're making too much of this. Isn't he doing better, I mean, you guys? Oh, Mom, please can't you just let it go?"

"I'm sorry, but I need to go now. I'm so sorry," I mumbled as I walked out the door around one p.m.

I felt crummy, sick to my stomach, and did not want to admit what I knew to be true. I climbed into my grey Jeep Cherokee, and the dogs looked forlornly out the front door as Paxton closed it. *He'll not be at our time-share or at the casino. Who am I trying to kid? He's at Lola's, but I'll be able to finally catch him in his web of lies.* He's supposedly the keynote speaker at an annual mayoral retreat in Ocean Shores, a coastal town south of our beach house and nearby casino. *Or was he? Maybe this provided a convenient excuse.* The lies and the excuses were floating in my head as I pulled out of the driveway.

Ruminating about my plan, I sped along, crossing bridges and familiar waterways on my way to the coast. *I don't want my thoughts to be true—or do I? This is like Groundhog's Day or Deja vu all over again (thanks, Yogi). No, it's March Madness. One year ago, almost to the day, I caught them together, and now I'm wildly driving to the beach, but he won't be there. Instead, they'll be back in Seattle in that same bed where I caught them before. Am I delusional?*

All these thoughts were running rampant as I drove on automatic pilot. Driving to the beach was second nature. In the past ten years since the Indian casino had been built, we had driven there often. If we did not have occupancy of our time-share, the casino paid for our room at their hotel because Alan was their biggest gambler, their VIP.

I resisted the temptation to call him on my cell, preferring instead to expose his lies. As I made the long climb up and through a steep forested highway, I pressed the pedal to the floor. *I'll show him I'm no fool.* My trusty jeep lurched and coughed and sputtered. I was in the middle of nowhere on a one-lane highway, closed in by the Olympic National forest. I could only go about ten miles per hour, and my car was shaking, but I felt I couldn't stop for fear of complete car failure. I did not have any cell reception, so calling Triple A would have been a bust.

I pulled way over to the white line onto a narrow shoulder, pushed on my hazard flashers and crept along. Pretty soon, a host of perplexed, impatient drivers formed a long line behind me. I was steadily driving in front of an angry mob, who were flashing their lights and honking their horns. I knew I was foolish for not pulling over and stopping, but I was over half-way there and in the middle of forested terrain. I ascertained that no driver could help me, nor did I want to take a chance of stopping my car. I was stubborn and determined, so I just kept chugging along, making desperate phone calls to Alan—to no avail.

As I got closer to Seabrook, but still in the forested corridor with occasional cell service, I called the hotel to see if he had checked in. He hadn't, but I learned that he did have a reservation, so my plan to catch him was intact (at least in my fantastical thinking).

My final attempt at contacting him proved to be more irrational. I called the casino and had him paged. I tensed like a stretched rubber band as the minutes ticked by. Ten long minutes later, a kind voice intoned, "I'm sorry, ma'am, but Alan hasn't responded."

"Uh, thanks." *Why am I doing this? I know where he is. I know what I'm going to find.* My mind was racing; my car was not.

All of a sudden, a black sedan came rushing by my side, evidently passing many cars to get to me. I saw his anger as he veered towards me in an attempt to run me off the road. I don't know how I managed to evade a major collision, but I pulled the wheel hard to the right, turning into a muddy field. I jumped out into the gunk in an attempt to figure out what happened and to get the license plate number, but the enraged driver had already sped away in disgust.

After the string of cars streamed by, I backed my car onto the road and crawled the rest of the way into Seabrook. *What a way to spend Easter. I need to have my head examined. Glad Megan is in Los Angeles with her cousin. She'd be livid. Poor Paxton, back home all alone on this holiday. What am I going to tell them this time?*

Though my jeep still bears the scars of that fateful day, mine have faded with time—time, the great healer.

As I limped into the parking lot of the casino hotel, flashing blue and red lights caught my eye. I pulled over and rolled down the window as the state trooper approached. "Ma'am, I was behind you back there on the highway and find it strange that you bypassed the service station."

"I, uh, I wanted to get here because my husband's here and I was afraid to stop. I'm parking at this hotel, and I'll have him help me," I blubbered. He probably thought I was crazy. Hell, I *was* crazy. My husband wasn't there. He was back in Seattle with his favorite mistress, choosing to forgo his greedy beach mistress. Too many choices—and I wasn't one of them.

I didn't think the officer would understand.

CHAPTER 33

An Exhibition of Bravery

OR A RECOGNITION OF COWARDICE...

The sea gulls circled overhead, making screeching cries. The neon lights blinked behind me, beckoning the gamblers. The sun flashed its pinks and golds, sinking deeper into the horizon as it dragged the day to a close. And I—I stood alone in the casino parking lot, making the phone call that would end my marriage.

Fumbling with my phone, I flipped it open and hit redial. It rang three times and, on the fourth—right before going to voicemail—he answered. "Uh, I know, I know; I just couldn't return your calls. I'm on my way now; I'm really sorry, Margy."

"So, you're on your way from Seattle, from Lola's? I was going to surprise you, but I guess the surprise is on me." Silence. "Why, Alan, why? It's Easter, for God's sake… couldn't you at least…"

More silence and then a seminal moment: "But I love her, Hon."

What was I supposed to say in response? Was I supposed to say: 'Well, all righty then, I understand. Why don't you turn around and pick her up. When you get here, we'll celebrate.'

The gulls had landed close to me, fighting over a half-eaten plate of nachos. Their shrieks punctuated the atmosphere. Gamblers were weaving through the lot towards the brightly lit casino. Easter was over. Darkness had descended. And I—I was trying to hang on to a shred, a few crumbs of dignity.

I exhaled. "Alan, my car's dead. I'm stuck at the casino hotel, or else I would get in it and drive back home and file for divorce tomorrow, you fuckin' asshole, you lying piece of shit. I even asked you on our walk this morning if you were struggling." Another exhale. "God, I'm so stupid."

"I'm so conflicted. I'm really sorry. I'll be there in about an hour. We'll deal with your car…uh, Margy, I didn't want it to happen like this. Sorry."

I snapped the phone shut and walked across the lot to the hotel where I checked-in under his reservation. The concierge had the nerve to ask, "Is Alan at the casino?" He was their VIP, so they wanted to make sure he was gambling. *What a sickness!*

I headed back across the parking lot, grabbed my bag from the car and locked it. The gulls and gamblers had moved on.

When I arrived in my hotel room, I felt claustrophobic, so I opened the curtain, unlocked the slider, and stepped out onto the deck. The hypnotic voice of the ocean calmed me. It strengthened my resolve. *I've been made the fool.* I had been wasting my life on the back burner where I simmered for years—a slow burn. Though my world was about to be turned upside down, the recognition of my cowardice was about to become an exhibition of bravery.

I breathed in the salty ocean air and wrestled with my thoughts. I had been proud of holding on, of keeping the family together. *But,* I reasoned as I leaned out over the railing, *the only thing I'm holding on to is my own misery.* I was not filled with wracking grief or even close to tears. In fact, I was pulling out arrows from my quiver when I heard the door click open.

Resentment sizzled in my veins as I turned from the serenity of the ocean and came into the room.

Alan's face flushed crimson red when we made eye contact. He sat on the edge of the floral bedspread and put his head in his hands.

Still trying to work all the angles (I guess some habits die hard), he pleaded, "Please, don't make this hard for me. I didn't plan it…it's complicated. I love both of you, actually. I'm so torn."

No longer concerned about saving my marriage or my dignity, I let him have it, flinging words across the space of years. Relishing in my control, I became emboldened by my bravado, prosecuting my case and spewing venom. "How's your son?" I taunted. "Lola doesn't even know what Woodstock is—or Vietnam— she wasn't even born." I scoffed as I pounded my palm on the desk. "Do you even know her politics? You make me sick."

He just sat there taking it, not offering any rebuttal. Though he deserved every piercing accusation, I took no responsibility for my part; instead, I became the character deserving sympathy, the likable victim in this story. Life is not that one-sided, not that black and white, but losing all perspective for one last night rescued me from thirty years of loneliness.

My words were like punches, landing many blows. "You'll never walk your daughters down the aisle. You'll never see my family, my brother—who treated you like a brother—you'll never see or talk to him again. Your friends—who are my friends—what were you thinking? Are you crazy? How can you love someone who was willing to lie and cheat your family?"

I caught my breath. "The pets—Spanky and Tucker and the cats—you'll never see them again. Don't even try. You disgust me. You stole my life, robbed your family of happiness…for what? So, you could sneak around with a woman who could be your daughter? Stringing me along for all those years. Why?"

Finally, he lifted his head from his hands. "Please, stop. I didn't mean to fall in love… I didn't plan it…I love my family, too…I just, Christ, it's exhausting. Do you think we could get some sleep? I have an important presentation in the morning."

I walked back onto the deck and listened to the roar of the ocean. The crescent moon hung in the dark sky, and I felt the rhythm of the tides and smelled the salt-laced air. Though my world had been turned upside down, the sun would come up tomorrow, the sea gulls would glide on the wind, gamblers would continue to roll the dice...

Life would go on.

Chapter 34

Side Effects

A SCORNED WOMAN SHOULD COME WITH A WARNING LABEL...

After deciding to end my marriage, I should have had a warning label stamped on my forehead because the early stage of divorce reads much like the side effects of a Cialis commercial:

"Filing for divorce gives you the chance to hurry up and wait... divorce may cause outbursts of anger, crying jags, and crazy, irrational thoughts. When contemplating divorce, be sure to not drink alcohol in excess for erratic behavior like cutting your ex out of all the family photos and throwing his dirty underwear on the porch of his long-term mistress might ensue. Other symptoms may include self-pity, self-absorption, and self-destruction. If any of these behaviors lasts more than four hours, get out of the bathtub and call a friend right away. Hell, call a gaggle of girls because this requires immediate attention."

The rows of pink and red camellias were bursting from their buds as Alan turned up our lane. On the long drive home from the beach, I continued to rant and rave—ugly accusations— deserved, but ugly. He, on the other hand, implored me not to do anything rash. "Margy, just leave a few bags of clothes in the courtyard for me to pick up after work. I'll be at the Hilton. Please, don't do anything crazy."

I slammed the passenger door. "Have a nice life."

Hilton, my ass, and a few bags of clothes. How about thirty years' worth of memories all stuffed into plastic bags?

I walked down the brick pathway, leading to the front door. When I opened it a crack, Spanky nudged his big head through and greeted me with a wet slurp. Not far behind, his sidekick, Tucker, joined us in a love fest. "Come on boys, we've got work to do."

I now believe in the stories where adrenaline can propel a mother to lift up a car to save her baby…or rush into a burning house…or bag up thirty years of clothes…

Flinging open the mirrored sliders, I started to purge him from my life. In went the laundered shirts, the Ralph Lauren light wool suits, the slippery silk ties, the knit ties, and the Scottish wool ties. In went his tennis attire, his golf shirts, his bike pants, his rain gear, and all his Joseph A. Banks cashmere sweaters. I carried at least fifty bags to the courtyard within thirty minutes. After a while, I quit bagging, and much like a jilted lover in a romance movie, I just started throwing his shoes and underwear into the courtyard.

The dogs thought it was great fun, nosing around all the bags, but then Paxton pulled up, and my adrenaline plunged.

"Mom, what the hell is this? You're not getting a divorce tomorrow, are you? This is Dad's house, too. It looks so trashy…and…and you guys seem so immature…I don't know how to handle this." She ran crying into her bedroom—nearly broke my heart.

I needed to calm down and have some semblance of sanity for my daughter's sake, but I *wanted* to act immaturely, I *wanted* to vent, and I needed to purge the house of everything Alan. Paxton had witnessed our separation a year before, and she knew her dad had "made his own bed"; however, she had been led to believe that we were a family again, and Lola was in the past. She was angry and sad and confused. She was thrust into a role she had never bargained for: my protector.

It was the worst of times, but in some ways, it was the best of times.

Paxton and Megan were young adults when Alan and I divorced. Many books are written about how divorce affects younger children, but not nearly as much attention is paid to adult children of divorce. My girls were expected to understand, to suck it up because they were adults. I saw firsthand how adversely affected they were for a myriad of reasons. First and foremost, they had their two parents together, as a family, through all their formative years. They had stability, and then the rug was pulled out from under them just as they were embarking on their adult journeys. Secondly, the expectations placed on them were overwhelming. Overnight, their world was turned upside down and their loyalties were severely tested. Divorce has become a defining event in my daughters' lives, affecting their decisions, attitudes, and even their happiness, even though it's been ten years in the rearview mirror.

I was leashing the dogs for a walk to pick up my car when Paxton came out of her room. "Mom, can I walk with you? We can talk. Besides, I don't want to be here when Dad picks up his stuff."

That evening he called. "Well, I guess you've made up your mind. Please don't run out tomorrow and file for divorce. Please, if you want, I could come home and we could talk about it. I think I could get over Lola."

"God, Alan, you sound like a stuck record. No, no, and no. Why can't you just let me go with some dignity? Why? This is really maddening. What is it? Really, you are pathetic. I don't want to be married, so what am I supposed to do…live in limbo?"

"Uh, please don't file for divorce. I, I, well, I have been financially irresponsible. Filing for divorce will hurt you too; there will be major consequences."

I slammed the phone into its holder. I had no idea what financial consequences awaited me, nor did I care. I was done.

For the next month, I purged. I opened every closet, cleaning out the wounds and bearing witness to things exactly as they were, including my own part in the pain. Uncluttering our house helped cut a path to my deeper self.

What were the heavy things that kept getting in the way? My past? His past? Or just the truth about life? It is messy and complicated. The realistic answer is that the past, present and future all lie together in a huge heap, one affects the other.

My past, his past, they were all there in the closets and like Pandora's box, scraps of memory came tumbling out—the brown grocery sacks stuffed with hospital bills and insurance benefit sheets... *she was a million-dollar baby...*the heartbeat tape, the ultrasound picture sent lovingly to me by Megan's biological mom. *Thirteen miscarriages. Did that day so many years ago, that day my son was conceived, have something to do with my inability to carry a baby? Was I being punished? No matter the answer, Megan and Paxton exist, and that is all that matters. Not how or why.*

I moved on to the next closet where I came upon my high school and college yearbooks and my scrapbooks full of yellowed newsprint and blue ribbons. There was one white ribbon prominently displayed on the fraying pages. I remember it well. *Fourth place out of thirty-two contestants in the district track meet as a freshman with no training and no encouragement. Just sheer guts.*

I opened the signing pages of my high school freshman yearbook...I found it...it was a message, a love letter of sorts, from my first boyfriend, an innocent but forbidden love because he was a Nez Perce Indian, gorgeous, and athletic...a senior. As I read his beautiful words, I went back to that innocent time. *We snuck around. Did goofy things and fantasized about being together. Prom, he didn't want to go with anyone else, so he didn't; instead, he came to my bedroom window, and we kissed through the screen. He went away to an Indian college in Kansas. I mourned but moved on. My senior year, he came back to the reservation. I saw him one last time. Alcohol and automobiles...he was killed trying to flag down a car. My dad wondered why I cried.*

I found the love letters...I had forgotten about Lieutenant Patrick O'Neil...my fling from a college trip abroad. One stop was West Berlin. I blushed as I read his romantic words...*leaving my college tour for a week to stay with a U.S. commissioned officer...that beer 'Haus' on the west side of the Wall...his brown eyes...his motorcy-cle...guess I wasn't such a 'cold fish' after all...*

Alan's memory books...his childhood pictures...his athletic awards. I found more brown sacks filled to the brim with losing lottery tickets, losing sports tickets. *Why on Earth would he save these?* Never dawned on me at the time...but now, I am guessing tax write-offs...doesn't matter...

Ten years ago, I was a survivor in transition, elevating the pain of the past, unable to let go. Today, I own the past, the present and look to the future, and I have endured to tell my story.

During the purge, I piled-up his belongings, his memories, his half of the estate, tossing in the family portraits. I topped the heap off with the black cement horse's head.

A month later, I filed for divorce.

Chapter 35

The Absurd World of Divorce

DIVORCE IS ITS OWN BREED OF CAT...

I had no expectations. Why would I? When I settled in the polished leather chair across from my lawyer, I had no understanding of the divorce process. So when my lawyer concluded that he was going to get me $11,000 a month in spousal support, and we were going to make a life plan, I sat back startled.

Throughout our marriage, I was never privy to my husband's earnings, but my lawyer, who sat only three feet away, looked me in the eyes and promised: "He's been a distinguished professor for over forty-two years, and he's been your family's breadwinner. You've been the family's home support. No judge is going to let your lifestyle drastically change." He continued, "And I can probably get this wrapped up in a month."

Wow, I was going to see $9,000 a month more than I had ever seen, and this would happen in a month. I floated out of his office, feeling like the luckiest divorcee on Earth!

That evening at Ladies' night, I could hardly wait for my tennis match to end.... *$11,000 a month...* Whack...*done in a month...* Smash. "Hey, Margy, you somewhere else tonight?"

"Oh, sorry, sorry, can't wait to get to our booth. Are we going to Quinn's or Watson's?"

185

"Let's go to Watson's; they have better wine and delicious oysters. Can't wait to hear about your first meeting."

We crowded together in our booth, and I began my story. "Well, you guys know that it took seven attempts to find a lawyer. No one wanted my case. They all knew Professor Alan and wouldn't touch it. Many had been his students."

"Oh, these divorce lawyers are big chickens. I had to fire my divorce lawyer because he wouldn't stand-up to Drew. I would be leery, Margy."

"Lucky number 7 took my case because he doesn't know Alan; he's heard of him…but seems undaunted by fame. He seems to know what he's talking about. I think I'm going to do just fine." *The lawyer said he would have this wrapped up in a month. Surely, my case won't be like theirs.*

But my divorced friends, my best friends, would not be dissuaded. "I've heard of your lawyer, Margy. He's in the same firm as the lawyer I used when I divorced Keith," another friend added. "I hated my lawyer. He liked Keith better than me; it was obvious. I send him a check every month for $25 because he made me so mad and charged so much. I'm paying the balance on the twenty-year plan."

Raw and naive, I sat listening while my friends regaled me with more horror stories about their divorces. One ex-husband came into my friend's house uninvited and prowled around. When she returned, she found art missing from the walls. Each one of my friends felt that they had been lied to about their husbands' assets and finances. When our Pinot Grigios and Syrahs were set before us, we clinked glasses. "Cheers." Then my friends got down to business.

"Look, Margy, whatever you do, get rid of your high-priced lawyer. They have no incentive to push for a quick divorce. They don't make money if they settle quickly. It's a racket and that's why the reputation fits."

"But, guys, my divorce attorney is different…" I stammered.

"Oh, Good Lord," my savvy divorced friend exclaimed while motioning to our favorite bartender. "Denise, could you get Margy another Pinot Grigio as soon as humanly possible."

Crash landing. A month went by and nothing happened. I appeared at the lawyer's office to talk to the assistant as to the progress, or lack thereof. "It's my lunch half-hour, walk with me to the deli, we can talk."

A block later we arrived, and she grabbed a soup and sandwich to go. We walked back up the street towards her office. Silly me, I thought we might have a conversation over a cup of tortilla soup. As we wove through the noon-time rush, she divulged that my ex-to-be had not disclosed a piddly thing, so they were getting tough with him. They set a hearing for temporary support.

"Great, when?"

"Well, when he discloses." I felt as if I were in an Abbott and Costello dialogue… *Who's on First?*

"Huh, how is that helpful to me? I still have to beg for monthly support while you guys wait until he discloses his financial secrets." I was frustrated that I was not informed about this process and that my lawyer and assistant didn't have any urgency. I was just another client who could flap in the wind while they played by the divorce handbook, and I sat on the bench.

"That's how it works." As the elevator door opened, she walked in. I had no idea I would be billed for an hour.

They sent a second letter, demanding that he disclose his assets and debts. He was so far ahead of them, he probably roared with indignation. Although Alan had never practiced law, he taught it and knew all the laws of discovery, he wasn't about to disclose any skeletons. We were at a stalemate. I discovered that divorce attorneys made money by the minute. If I phoned the legal assistant and talked for five minutes, I got charged for a quarter hour. Like a homemaker who saves up jobs before calling a plumber, I started to save up all my concerns, questions, and "yeah, buts" before I called my lawyer.

Divorce is its own breed of cat with its own language and set of laws that only a divorce attorney indulges. What added to my difficulty, many times over, was the fact that my husband acted as his own attorney and didn't appreciate divorce law or precedence, but he knew the law well enough to use it to his advantage. He didn't care that the meter was running for me. He cared only about protecting his intimidating position and financial secrets. He stalled and would not respond. He used to say to me when in a new competitive arena: "There's a new sheriff in town." Divorce soon became the new sheriff, and he brought along his deputy, the Piper. Alan was going to have to pay.

I did my best to inform my lawyer of our assets, but I didn't know the plain and simple truth. There were no assets; they had been gambled away. We had been living a lie, living way beyond our means. Surely, our ranch house, an acre lot overlooking the Green River we had purchased for $150,000 in 1980, would give me security if I had to sell it. I was soon to learn the overwhelming truth. Desperate to cover his lavish lifestyle of wine, women, and craps, he had refinanced our family home six times over the course of fifteen years. He had used our house like an ATM machine.

How, one might ask, did he do that without my knowledge? He forged my name, taking me off the deed. I learned this when I started doing my own divorce research. Unable to get any straight answers, I called a realtor from a reputable firm in the area. As we were doing a walk-through of my house, she relayed a horrifying circumstance. "When you called this morning, I quickly pulled up the information on your house, and I don't believe you have knowledge of this." She showed me the document. "Is this your signature?"

"Oh, my God, no. Not even close. How could he do this?" I felt like I had been punched in the gut, and I welled-up with tears, unable to comprehend the betrayal.

The realtor surmised, "My guess is he had a shady notary and greedy loan officer, all wanting to take advantage of the housing bubble."

Reality hit me. Built in 1947, my charming house with a sweeping vista from every room, the only home my children and animals had ever known, could not be sold for the price of my husband's last loan, procured in 2007. In the down-turned market of 2008, the year of my divorce, my house could not even sell as a tear-down because builders were going bankrupt. Developers were not even interested in an acre of prime property.

The grim picture was becoming clearer and clearer as I looked over the loan statement and the forged deed the realtor had left in my possession—I no longer existed. He was the sole owner.

This juicy piece of wrongdoing went right to the top of my list as I dialed my lawyer. "No wonder he won't disclose any documents. He forged my name and took me off the deed to our house. What's going to happen? We can't go into court with this information, can we? Don't we have him over a barrel?"

"His barrel may be bigger. If this gets reported, his reputation will be ruined, and he could lose his senior professorship. What is he going to do? Sell shoes at Nordstrom's?" I felt like I was reappearing in another episode of Abbott and Costello, comparing whose barrel was bigger.

"Look," he continued, "there are two ways to go with divorce. If there are considerable assets, you split those fifty/fifty, and no spousal support long term, or you go after his labor and get spousal support for life."

He hesitated. "You have no choice but to go for the latter."

"But he's getting—"

"You're asking me to make chicken salad out of chicken shit."

And I was.

CHAPTER 36

Hope

A FEELING YOU DON'T KNOW YOU HAVE UNTIL IT'S GONE.

Hope. It's a funny thing, different from all the rest. It's not like love or fear or hate. It is a feeling you don't really know you have until it's gone.

There I sat, staring at my computer screen in my extra-large plaid pajamas, half-drunk on a $3.99 bottle of Pinot Grigio. Eight months into the divorce process, while I was learning on the job, I found myself running out of hope. Wave after wave of nausea washed over me.

The credit report staring back at me did not lie.

I was back in the all-purpose room—a room with sponge-painted, tie-dyed walls and a turquoise cement floor—this room was a reminder of the many phases and stages of my life. It had been the room where all the memory books were stored. The dogs had slept on the smelly couch pushed-up against the psychedelic wall. At one time, it had been the sewing room where I had made my own clothes; the machine was still stashed in the corner, gathering cobwebs. It had been the nursery for Paxton and her night nurse; the respiratory machine still lingered on the counter. It had been the toy room where my girls had played house. The room had finally become Divorce Central with stacks of legal documents and unpaid bills. It had become the computer room where all my emails going back and forth with my lawyer were stored.

But that night, everything changed. The room where everything seemed possible became the place where I lost all hope.

Early in the divorce, when gathering financial information about our assets, I learned the ugly truth that Alan had taken me off the deed, and he had become the sole owner. During the divorce process, he had agreed to quick deed the house back to me, and if I sold it, I would receive all the profit. But I refused. Against my lawyer's advice, I would not take the deed back because I didn't trust Alan, and I didn't want to sell it either because I was staying put! At that chaotic time, I had no understanding of Alan's financial collapse, and naively, I believed he would keep paying the mortgage.

The only route out of my house—my home for thirty years—would be a body bag. It remained the last link to the self I had once been. My house reflected my life—haphazard, chaotic, and broken, but it was also charming, eclectic, and authentic.

I had loved that house from the moment I walked into the entry and stepped onto the hardwoods. Straight in front of me, framed by two huge windows, stood Mt. Rainier. Every morning I found solace in the orange and pink sunrise climbing over the snow-capped mountain. At night, through those picture windows, I would glimpse the waxing and waning of the moon. Every so often, those big windows would produce a masterpiece—a full harvest moon.

Although figuring out how to hold on to my beloved house had become a constant worry, the idea of selling it was unthinkable. No one, except my girls and me, could understand why I was hanging onto a 1947 run-down ranch house that needed major repairs and was probably best as a tear-down.

I had taken on all the responsibility to save myself; no one else was going to save me. I had accepted that I was not going to live a linear life, wrapped in the loving arms of a husband. I had accepted the break-up of our family and the loss of a long-term marriage. I had even accepted my failures, but when it came to my house, I would not take off the rose-colored glasses. Through those glasses, I held on to hope—a sense of the possible and a way to preserve the past. Through those glasses, I glimpsed the good times, the funny times, and the lovely times as a family.

The Pollyanna in me thrived and those glasses provided wishful thinking.

Over the years, I went through different decorating phases and a palette of paint colors; I staged my life, making lasting memories. Before children, my friend and I painted almost every wall throughout the house an egg-shell blue. While we were painting the living room, where the big windows offered a view of the river, we saw something floating in the dark water. My friend got the binoculars and yelled for me down the hall. "Margy, hurry in here; I see a body... ooh."

Soon, the river patrol was there, blinking its red and blue lights. We shared the binoculars and reported to one another: "They're pulling him out; he's bloated. What a hairy back."

"Just think, at one time, he was someone's baby boy," my friend said. This line sticks with me to this day.

I went through my wallpaper phase, papering in plaids, flowers, and grass-cloth. When the girls were about twelve, we left them home alone while we went to Las Vegas. Megan called me on the last day. "Mom, just warning you, please don't get mad, but I have ripped all the wallpaper off the family room walls."

"What?"

"Don't worry. I'm painting it a dark blue. I'll be done before you get home."

I walked in to midnight blue, unprofessionally painted. That next week, I repainted it a teal blue and, with Megan's suggestion, added some white shutters, which started my next phase—every room would have a different palette and a new personality. I painted the entry hall a deep cranberry; it took four coats. I learned that red colors don't cover as well, just the opposite of what I intuited. From the cranberry entry, one would enter into the Mediterranean pink living room. From there, one would step into my bright yellow ranch kitchen. What was I thinking? I wasn't, but I loved it and have stellar memories from those eccentric years.

Most notably were the pictures taken one Christmas with the pink walls as the backdrop. We always had a rip-roaring card game, complete with everyone's handle and prizes for first, second, and last. Alan had come up with a brilliant idea for the prizes. First prize would be a snapshot taken with our beloved retriever mix, Spanky. Second prize would be taken with our little Shih-Tzu, Tucker, and the booby prize would be taken with Alan. My brother, who adored Spanky, came in first. My dad came in second, and I have memorialized the picture of him holding Tucker, both grinning from ear to ear. But the best remains the picture of my mom, arm-in-arm with Alan. Probably the only time they would be photographed together with a smile.

Running the length of our house was a brick patio that overlooked the river. One day when we had first moved in, I noticed that one brick had a crack, and in its fissure, grass had grown, just perfect for a golf tee. To hit over the river would take a monstrous three-hundred-yard drive, so we figured the houses across the way were safe. Years and years of parties, where fierce competitions ensued, yielded years and years of fun—and even a blurb in the local newspaper, until a few college golfers took their turn, driving ball after ball on to the deck of a house across the river.

The next day, a couple came walking up our brick path, holding a bag of golf balls. They asked us to cease and desist. "We feel as though we're looking down the barrel of a gun. We feel we need to wear helmets in order to sit on our deck."

Oh, what memories!

When our children were babies, we bought an organ that played by plugging a computer chip into a slot. Our girls grew up dancing and singing in our living room. They would entertain us, singing to tunes ranging from Frank Sinatra's *New York, New York* to Dolly Parton's *Big Rock Candy Mountain*. They even tapped on the hardwood. Megan became an accomplished dancer, dancing with a company for many years. She is now a dance teacher. Paxton still bears the nickname her cousins had given her from years of singing. To them, she will forever be Tunes. I take pause and remember Megan's first twirls, her first bows, her first pas-de-deux on pointe while Tunes crooned to Patsy Cline—memories made—all in that joyous front room.

On the advice of my friends, I had pulled up a free credit report and what lay before me dashed my dreams and hopes. My rose-colored glasses smashed, and I began to sob, wiping tears and snot on the sleeve of my well-worn cashmere sweater. I could not save my house. The numbers I saw did not even make sense, weren't even real. Would I have to leave my house?

Alan had not been forthcoming about his last loan. He had sucked all the equity out of the house. Not only that, but he was paying a mortgage far below the monthly interest. He had secured a loan known as negative amortization, so that the balance was increasing every month. Although Alan was paying the mortgage, there was the possibility that the bank would foreclose. I was confused and angry. Still, I was determined to stay put as long as possible.

Blood rushed to my head and my jaw throbbed from all the grimacing. *What kind of person places his family in such jeopardy?* I started to wander around my newly painted house. I had just painted every room a rich caramel, which made the artwork pop from the walls. I walked to the windows, looked at Mt. Rainier and marveled at the moon shining off of the river. I screamed. *What kind of human never thought about his family? Never planned for the future, but instead, guaranteed there would be no future?*

Hope. It's a funny thing. It is a feeling you don't really know you have until it's gone.

CHAPTER 37

Tarnished Silver

CRISIS FORCES CHANGE...

Life is ever-changing.

All around us there is proof—our bodies change with the ravages of age; relationships change with love, lost or found; babies change into images of ourselves; beaches and mountains change with the erosion of time—and on and on it goes. Yet, few of us accept change readily; preferring, instead, to hunker down, ignoring the incoming tide.

One year later, I was divorced. During the turbulent year, I had tried to sell my house; I had scraped and scrapped and even borrowed from my dad to pull the possibility together, but to no avail. So, I decided I was staying put for as long as possible. With hindsight, I see that I refused to alter or change my life in any meaningful way. I chose to stay lodged in unhappiness, clinging to my house; I chose to be a prisoner in my own home, living life in miniature.

I had been so attuned to living in silhouette, I had forgotten what life felt like underneath. Like a tree covered in moss or a piece of tarnished silver, my reality was hidden. I needed a storm to blow away the moss; I needed to scratch off the tarnish in order to shine.

I needed a crisis to force change, and one day it came flying up my driveway.

I was pulling weeds in my yard in the late spring after my divorce when an old blue Chevy, piled high with manila folders, came to an abrupt stop. A middle-aged woman rolled down her window and smoke came billowing out. "Mind if I take a few pictures?" she asked. "Are you living here? Renting?"

I got off my knees and stood up. "Ma'am, I'm the owner. I have lived here for thirty years."

"Hmmmm…I represent the bank that owns your house. I'm part of the foreclosure unit."

I approached her car and leaned down to eye level. "Oh, I can explain; you see my ex-husband took out a loan; he's paying the mortgage so I can live here." *He was paying the mortgage, wasn't he?* "It's complicated, but I think you are mistaken. I would appreciate it if—"

"Hey, I was married to one of those, too. One of those liars; I'm sorry, but I have to do my job. Is that your daughter who just came out?"

I was baffled. Why was the foreclosure lady here, asking all these questions? I gulped, "Yes. Why?"

"Could you ask her to step aside? The bank doesn't want kids in the picture, just proof of cars and that someone lives here."

"She's a young adult. I just don't understand; really, this is upsetting. Why wouldn't I have been told? Um… are we living here illegally?" I imagined us being kicked out. Where will we go? Was Alan lying again?

"The way the housing market is today with all the backlog, all the foreclosures, I'd say you have six months before the bank kicks you out." Six months…and then what happens? What happens if we refuse to leave?

She snapped a few pictures and hopped back in her car. "You take care, Honey, I've been there."

She drove around the circle and was off to her next job.

God, I'm a squatter in my own home. I put the rake back in the shed, rounded up the dogs, who had been romping around in the lower yard, and went inside where I knew an explanation would be due. Where, I knew, I would have to confront our reality. We were essentially homeless, hanging on by a slender thread, which was growing thinner with each passing month. *When will the bank take charge and foreclose? When will I need to get my prized possessions out of the house before the sheriff comes to repossess? Why won't I go? When should I go? Where should I go?*

"Mom, what was that all about?" Paxton asked as she sat down at the square oak table. "Since we couldn't sell the house, I thought it was ours."

"Well, we can't live here any longer. The bank owns this house."

She jumped out of her chair, "What? Mom, you can't be serious." She was distraught, losing everything—her childhood home, two divorced, unstable parents…her future. It was all too much.

"Hey, let's look at it as an adventure. You knew we'd have to leave someday. Let's check Craigslist and go out looking for houses this weekend. Maybe there will be—"

"Come on, Mom. Who's going to let us bring four animals into a house? We'll have to hide Spanky."

"These are desperate times for sellers and owners. I sense opportunity." I had no idea what I was talking about, but I tried to stay positive.

She walked away down the hallway to her bedroom, and I stood gazing out the sliding glass door at the houses across the river, pondering many hard truths. I had tried to put a positive spin on our future, but losing my house and breaking my daughter's heart—all in one day—nearly killed me. Besides my daughter, I couldn't bear what might become of my animals. It was their home, too. Thank God Megan had moved to her own apartment; she couldn't even talk about losing her childhood home.

I'll fondly remember how this old ranch house has been Spanky's domain. I had never worried about him needing to go outside because, whenever he wanted, he would exercise his options. A regular Houdini, he would press his snout on the handle of the slider that led outside to the brick patio. With a swipe of his nose, the door would open, and he would meander out to survey his surroundings. If the door was locked, he would go to the laundry room, stick his big paw through the jerry-rigged cat door and pull; the marred door would swing towards him, and he would trot onto the brick path, leading to the pond. If the doors were closed after his departure, he would circle around to the front door and bust through, pressing his barrel chest against the door until it gave way. Whenever, I would hear his pitter-patter on the wooden parquet floor, I would announce, "Spanky's home." He didn't seem to mind which door he accessed. I found it amusing and comforting. *I will sorely miss his routine.*

The animals were curled-up together on their large doggy bed, and I was alone with my thoughts. I lowered my body to the cool tiles on the kitchen floor, went into the fetal position and started to weep. My sorrowful wails awoke Spanky, who came quietly to lie down by my side. He put his giant paw on my shoulder and licked the tears from my face. Somehow, I knew, we were going to be okay.

My pity party ended that day.

Alan had continued to pay the mortgage even though the house was underwater, meaning that he owed more on the house than it was worth. But Alan had neglected to tell me the mortgage would balloon to $7,000 a month, and he would stop paying. Honestly, I would have stopped paying, too, but it would've been nice to know before the foreclosure lady had pulled into our circular driveway.

Every one of my friends and family had an opinion, and I felt pulled in all directions: "Go now; never give up; you probably have a year; maybe they'll come next week."

When I finally accepted the truth, though my house was being unjustly taken from me, I astonished myself with my resilience and

courage to change. For several months, I busied myself in construc-
tive ways. Paxton and I went out searching for houses to rent, and
I set a date certain for my two-day moving sale.

Instead of dwelling on the past, I embraced the future.

I spent weeks organizing my big moving sale, weeding out thirty
years of life, deciding what to sell and what to keep. Within the
month, I turned almost every room and patio into a variety store.
I hung long rods from the rafters in the garage, turning it into the
clothing section. I marked, hung, and folded my daughters' hip
clothing they had outgrown or no longer wanted: the distressed
pairs of jeans, the one-time-occasion dresses, the unworn shirts and
shoes. I added to the mix: the big shoulder jackets from the eighties,
the fake fur coat, and outdated tennis wear. I even put my wedding
dress up for sale. Megan claimed it looked like a hippy dress with
the muslin beige material and lacy bell-bottom sleeves, so it would
never be worn again, anyway.

I washed and ironed all the linens. *I never use table linens anymore, so might as well sell them*, I decided. I did keep an embroidered
white linen tablecloth that Alan had brought back from Vietnam,
but it hangs, alas, gathering dust in the coat closet of my new home.
I polished many silver dishes, ones that had come from my grand-
mother, ornate and high-maintenance—with initials of my ancestors
engraved on them. As a wedding gift, we had received a pure silver
pitcher that had a thick layer of tarnish from many years of neglect.

When my friends, who were helping me with the sale, came to
help set-up, one remarked: "I'm not going to let you sell those silver
dishes, especially that pitcher."

"Why? I'll never use them."

"Trust me. You'll thank me someday." Though I didn't believe
her, I put the silver aside. Maybe she's right, I thought, I may want
a few nice pieces from my past.

The living room began to take shape as a toy store—all the
American dolls and furniture, the books, the wooden puzzles, the
games, the musical instruments no longer coveted or played, the

electric train set that had circled our Christmas tree every year... They all evoked memories, but I wasn't going to move them, so I asked my daughters' permission to sell their childhood with the understanding that they would receive a cut of the sale.

For young adults, money talked more than dolls.

When I was clearing out a back closet, I found Paxton's guitar. *She took one lesson and was done...gee, how many years has it been?* No time to stop and ponder. I slapped a $25 sticker on it and brought it out, propping it up against a chair so it would stand out. My two cats came over, sniffed the opening, and then sat like sphinxes, staring at the guitar.

At first, I didn't pay much attention and went about making my displays. I walked back in the room, and both were still fixated. I thought it was strange, so I observed them for a few more minutes. *There must be a mouse or some small rodent inside,* I thought. Upon that realization, I tipped the guitar upside down and out rolled a coiled snake—a big one. I carefully picked it up with a rake and threw it outside.

I never told the kid that his new guitar had once housed a snake because I didn't want to tarnish his magical moment.

Alan had collected ball caps, hundreds of hats, over the course of thirty years. I had displayed them on hooks, sometimes three-deep, in our mudroom. Our mudroom was also home to our wine shower. For Alan's Christmas present one year, I had our friend build cedar shelving inside the shower—-enough shelving for 250 bottles of wine. I was inspired while touring the Sonoma wine country when our guide told us that a fancy temperature-controlled cellar was not necessary—-all that was needed was an inside enclosure with no exposure to sunlight or outside walls. The mudroom shower was perfect; we never used it for showering, and when the wine bottles got dusty, all I had to do was turn on the shower. When Alan left, he took only a few hats, but he took all of the wine—what a deal! He left me with hats of many colors and many themes, and one in particular became a family heirloom.

It seemed like the "shit-head" hat had always been with us. I don't remember how it came into the collection, but it was hideous. The cap was a mustard yellow with a brown bill. Perched on the bill sat a plastic pile of poo; one could almost imagine steam rising from it. The slogan embroidered on the cap in big bold letters read: Shit-head. When we first had the hat, it was a novelty, and we had to wear it when we made a mistake. The kids got a kick out of this, but lost interest after our Golden Retriever, Jack, took a bite out of the replicated poo (must have looked authentic to him). I decided to part with our heirloom at my moving sale, adding it to the hat display.

An hour before the stated time of the moving sale, garage sale experts and enthusiasts were milling around the courtyard. Nobody prepared me for all the characters and the art of deal-making. A circus-like atmosphere ensued, and I let the party begin. I had put beer and wine on ice in a big barrel. Neighbors, friends, family, and strangers were soon intermingling and snapping up the bargains. The jewelry-lady zeroed in on a gold bracelet, a sportsman bought my daughter's fifteen-speed bicycle, a Beatles fanatic bought all my cherished albums…and on and on it went for two solid days. The linens were gone, the books, the toys, the dolls…the clothes were picked over, and some young teens made a haul. Though my wedding dress never sold, it made for interesting conversation. Guess I was a hippy. Who knew?

The day after the sale was moving day. Paxton and I had found a perfect rental, and yes, we had had to hide Spanky in order to make the deal. Fortunately, the landlord lived out of town, and when needed, I would hide Spanky in the car which I would park a mile away.

My daughter and I had determined to make our animals a priority when choosing our transitional rental house. Not an easy task as we had suspected. Very few owners rented to people with one dog, let alone two dogs (one who was over a hundred pounds) and two cats. It was, however, the fall of 2009, and the housing bubble had burst. Everyone was desperate, so we lucked into a 2500 square foot home in suburbia. Right outside our back gate sat two well-managed tennis courts. Spanky and I were in hog heaven!

The house was along an electrical corridor, providing a meadow and walking paths that all my pets, daughter and I enjoyed. Every morning, I would take Spanky and Tucker to the meadow as the dawn was breaking. To my pleasant surprise, the orange and pink sunrise would climb over Mt. Rainier. Every evening, I would repeat the process and glimpse the waxing and waning of the moon. And in those three years, I was blessed and feasted my eyes upon a full harvest moon.

My friends and I had organized the unsold goods into a pile for Goodwill. A week later, after settling into my transitional rental, I returned for a final reckoning—and a reckoning it was. All my handiwork sat in one huge pile. The neatly folded clothing, the hats, the unsold artwork—even the unsold bricks and white-picket fencing—all were askew in one messy heap. My pride of ownership was topped off by the shit-head hat. Guess that was fitting.

The Woodhaven saga was over.

I walked down the brick pathway, turning my back on the chaos that had been my life.

Chapter 38

Spanky's Legacy

WHAT MY DOG TAUGHT ME ABOUT LOVE AND LETTING GO

"When life gives you lemons, make lemonade." It is a simple idea about handling life's disappointments. Life is not fair, but it does offer the unending capacity to make the best of what we are given. Humans struggle with accepting this universal truth; dogs do not. In fact, our canine companions teach us how to take life head-on—how to love and let love, how to age with grace and dignity, and finally, how to let go.

Within the first month of living in our new rental in Sunrise Hill where the doors and locks all worked and the backyard was fenced and gated, Spanky showed his displeasure and asserted his control. He had been used to doors opening upon his command, and he was not going to let a few gates get in his way. He would not be denied access to his house. My daughter was away working, and I had my first substitute teaching job of the year. On a clear sunny day in September, I felt a sense of security to have all the pets contained in their new backyard.

Eight hours later, I came home to a disaster. Spanky must have gone right to work after my departure, for his destruction was monumental. First, I saw the open gate, then I saw the open door. Upon closer examination, both were in shambles, pulverized to wood chips and splinters. With further investigation, I cobbled together the following scenario: Unable to open the slider on the back deck, Spanky had circled to the side gate, expecting it to open. He, no doubt, put his big snout in between the slats, jiggled the gate and surveyed the situation. Next, he brought out his better weapons, his gigantic paws and teeth. Clawing and chewing his way through the slats, he freed himself and stood only a few yards from his front door.

The front door was a solid wooden door, secured by a deadbolt lock. This needed major artillery. I am guessing he spent hours chewing, clawing, and prying off the whole door jamb before calmly walking through and taking his rightful place on his Asian rug in the front room.

His tail thumped when I climbed through the opening. Like posing for a picture, he held his head high and smiled at me as if to say, *"Hi, Mom, aren't you proud of me?"*

I grabbed one of the pulverized pieces of wood and pointed it at him. "Spanky, bad, bad dog."

His tail thumped louder and he came towards me to give me a slurp. I kept pointing the stick. "Spanky…bad dog." *Thump, thump, thump, lick, lick, lick, whine, whine whine…* The anger and frustration melted away like foam, and soon I gave in to his enthusiastic embrace.

I rationalized that he had used his cunning and survival tools, which were as instinctual to him as his wolf ancestors thousands of years ago.

I rebuilt the gate, creating one from which even King Kong could not escape, and I had a cabinet and door company rebuild the door, but to be sure, I never, *ever*, kept Spanky from having access to his home again.

One major difference for all of us in Sunrise Hill was the experience of having a two-story house. In my entire life, I had never lived in anything but a ranch-style home. Every night, I enjoyed climbing the stairs away from all the distractions downstairs, entering my master suite for slumber only. I found much serenity in that process.

When we moved to Sunrise Hill, Spanky would quite nimbly climb the two flights of stairs and circle around his doggy bed, which sat on the floor at the foot of my bed. He would paw at his bed until it was just right. His nightly process gave me much comfort and joy.

By the third year, he struggled to climb the stairs, stopping on the landing to catch his breath and to rest his arthritic hips before attempting the last flight. Sometimes, he would arrive two hours after I was tucked in, plopping down noisily on his "unmade" bed. For three years, he never missed one night as my protector. However, I felt like I heard his internal dialogue, his wrestling with his predicament, and my comfort and joy slowly turned to sadness, hanging like a shroud around my heart.

In the last year of his life, his hind legs would sometimes cave under him, and he'd collapse in a heap onto the hardwood floor. With dignity, he would drag himself by his front paws over to the carpeted area where he could find enough stability to pull himself up again. He loved to greet callers at the door, but he would run excitedly from the carpeted area to the hardwood floor of the entrance, and when he greeted them, he would slide on his stomach out the door.

On one of those occurrences, a TV repairman looked horrified when Spanky had flopped around trying to find stability and fell out the door onto the porch at the repairman's feet. "Ma'am, is your dog dying?" he asked with a furrowed brow and round eyes.

"Oh, don't worry. He always does that. He'll right himself." I bent down and patted Spanky just to make sure. "Let me show you the TV. It's upstairs."

Pretty soon, we heard panting and saw a smiling red dog amble into the room. Spanky had just wanted to be part of the deal, and he sure as *hell* wasn't going to let a long staircase keep him from joining in.

Spanky and my dad were both in the twilight of their lives. My dad was approaching ninety-two and Spanky wasn't far behind in dog years. They were both grey and not very ambulatory. One major difference separated them, however: my dad was in the latter stages of dementia, but Spanky was as sharp as the day I brought him home as an eight-week-old pup. I agonized over both situations.

How ironic that I had a choice for Spanky, but not one for Dad. Several years earlier, my siblings and I moved Dad to Seattle to be closer to my sister and me. As my sister and I drove away from Dad's home, one we knew he would never see again, my heart sank. Dad was sitting in the back seat and tears were dripping down his sunken cheeks. He tapped me on the shoulder and bemoaned, "I had a great wife, and I've had a great life, now let me go."

Twice weekly, I would visit my dad in his memory care home. Though it was only a few miles from Sunrise Hill, I didn't go there every day because I came away too depressed. The smell of pee hit me as I walked through the door. Seasonal art projects taped to the windows reminded me more of a preschool class, than a home that housed once-proud doctors, lawyers, farmers, and teachers—that housed our mothers and fathers, wives and husbands.

Punching in the code to let me pass, I would walk into a sad reality of silver-haired men and women lined up staring at Dr. Phil, watching without audio from their recliners as aides brought around tiny cups of pills to keep them placid. Some slept slumped in their wheelchairs with a sandbag draped across their laps so they wouldn't fall out. Others carried around life-size dolls, talking to them like they were their babies. I stopped going at mealtimes because I could not bear to watch my dad dribble red Jello down the front of his cashmere sweater.

One sunny fall day, I took Spanky to visit my dad in the home, for even in his demented state, he would have moments of lucidity and ask, "How's Spanky?"

After punching in the code to escape, I wheeled Dad outside and locked his wheels while I went to retrieve Spanky. When I opened the car door, he leapt out and ran over to my dad, licking his face, whining loudly. My dad stared blankly and then the light of recognition for his old pal sprang into his eyes. Patting

Spanky's head, he lamented, "Well, there, old boy, I wish I could take you for a walk."

And in a way, his wish was granted. I unlocked the wheels to his chair, handed him the leash and off we went like a grand parade with Spanky proudly pulling my dad as I guided them from behind. *What a memory!*

Several days before my dad died, I found him all alone in his room, sitting in the dark, talking to himself. "I need to work the tractor today, Son. You take over the combine." *He's letting go. He's going back to his deepest roots—farm and family. He's passing the torch.* My heart wept but, as I tiptoed into the room, I had already accepted that no road is forever. *Good-bye, sweet Dad.*

I sat down beside him and put my hand in his. "Hi, Dad, it's Margy."

He held my hand for a long time before acknowledging me. "I know that."

He may not have known me at first, but as the visit progressed, it was obvious he had important words—important thoughts—he wanted to share. He must have been grappling with his faith and impending death. "Jesus came down on a long rope," he imparted and looked to me for affirmation.

I smiled. "That's amazing, Dad."

"He did, he really did."

I squeezed his hand. "I believe you, Dad." Interesting how humans need to believe there is more when death is imminent.

"I just want to go; I love you and want to help you…" *He knows who I am.* Relief washed over me like a fresh cool stream. I turned and gazed at him so he could see the light of gratitude beaming from my eyes. *What would I do without you? You care so much about my welfare and always have.*

Two days later, Dad quietly slipped into a coma and went to join Mom, fulfilling his long-awaited wish. His generosity and consideration for his children allowed me to realize my wish—a home of my own.

In the spring after Dad's death, I closed on an 1800 square foot home in stellar move-in ready condition. In fact, there were so many bells and whistles—air-conditioning, sprinkler systems, smoke alarms and doors that locked—I needed quite an adjustment period. I was slated to move in June. My dilemma: should Spanky make the move?

Both Paxton and I kept this concern to ourselves, but as the move loomed closer, we finally confided in one another. We were in the kitchen packing and the dogs were sleeping nearby. I turned from clearing a cupboard. "Penny for your thoughts. Do you think Spanky can make the move?"

"Mom, I can't make so many changes. Can we take a 'let's see' approach? I know he isn't going to live much longer, but I can't bear the thought of not having him. Please can we talk about this after we move?"

I smiled. *I love you.*

On the big move day, we boarded the two dogs at the kennel Two-Dog Night, a home-away-from-home for them both. As we unpacked and settled in my dream house, I became overwhelmed with sadness that Spanky would never be able to navigate or live comfortably in there. The whole downstairs living space was inlaid with Brazilian cherry hardwood and the sleeping arrangements involved two flights of stairs. I was torn. I had purchased the house knowing that Spanky was literally on his last legs, and yet, I wanted to make his final move, whatever that would be, comfortable. Before picking up the dogs that afternoon, I ran off to Target and bought five yoga mats in hopes to help Spanky stay upright when he walked into his new home.

As my daughter and I drove out to the kennel, unaccustomed silence filled the air like fog filling a valley. We kept to our own private thoughts. *I can't let him go yet. Maybe he can live another year. Am I being cruel? He drags that leg…he pants…Oh, God, I don't want to make this decision.*

Before they brought the dogs to us, the owner of the kennel pulled out his smart phone and showed me a picture. "You know he has a tumor protruding in the back of his mouth and it's making it painful to eat." He hesitated. "He had a heck of a time getting up from the floor."

With tears streaming down my face, I looked at him. "I know."

Both dogs howled and licked our faces, greeting us like we had been gone for months. We loaded them up in the jeep and headed for our last journey as an intact family.

Tucker, our little Shih Tzu, pranced through the door of his new home without a care in the world; Spanky, however, sniffed around every corner, approaching his new environment like a competent detective. I had placed his dog bed downstairs in the family room, so he wouldn't have to climb stairs in order to go to bed. That afternoon, Spanky had followed me from room to room, not letting me out of his sight, and I became cautiously optimistic.

As night fell, I tucked him into his bed and headed upstairs to mine. My daughter came running up the stairs. "Mom, Mom, Spanky's crying."

I went to the open stairwell and looked down. He was trying to climb the stairs, but could not even take the first step. Grabbing a down-comforter from the linen closet, I ran down the stairs where I slept on the leather couch, stroking his head throughout the night as he slept beside me.

When we woke up, I patted his greying muzzle. "Good morning, Spankers, time to get up and go outside." He looked at me with his big brown eyes and for the first time in his twelve-plus years, he growled at me. I knew that this day would be his last. He'd fought his last battle. *You will leave huge paw prints on my heart*, I thought as I reluctantly picked up the phone.

I called the vet and made the appointment for two that afternoon.

My new neighbors were outside visiting with one another on a sun-filled day. They waved and smiled at me, but they could see that I was weeping uncontrollably, so one of them came towards me to see what the matter was. I had been in the neighborhood less than twenty-four hours, so they all must have worried about what they had in store.

Through gulping sobs, I explained, "I have to put my dog down today."

One of the women put her hand on my back. "I'm so sorry...I'm Mary, by the way." She pointed toward my front door which had been left ajar. "Is that him?"

I turned to look. There stood Spanky with his head held high and two tennis balls in his mouth. He had managed to get his arthritic hips up and now he was ready to go. He had no idea today would be his last.

Spanky ambled into our circle in the middle of the cul-de-sac and fell down at our feet, placing his paws on top of his tennis balls. "He's so beautiful, but it's obvious you're making the right decision," one of the men said, as Spanky began *flirting*, trying to get him to steal his ball.

When Spanky lifted his paw, gravity took one of the balls, and it rolled down the block. When he tried to get up to chase it, he struggled in visible pain. When he finally got up, the roughness of the pavement had scraped and bloodied his back legs.

My new neighbors hugged me and gave comfort the best they could, given they had known me for less than a day.

Megan came to say goodbye, bringing my ten-day old grandson with her. Spanky greeted her like he always had, whining and thumping his tail. Megan laid my grandson on the rug to have a moment with our beloved family dog. Spanky did not disappoint, sniffing and licking my grandson as if he were passing the torch— the torch telling him to promote the bond of family. Megan left, waving limply as she drove away, and I waved back in kind until they turned the corner. *One life ending and another just beginning.*

I walked back inside and laid my heavily burdened body beside Spanky. He licked at the strands of my soul. I put my arm around him and nuzzled him, letting my memories carry me back in time... *you were the smartest, the most powerful dog I've ever had...you completed our family...loved us without pause...thank you.*

Jolting me from my walk down memory lane, Paxton came through the front door. "Mom, we've got to get this over with." *I know, I know. God, how?*

Using a tennis ball to get Spanks up, I kept it in front of his nose while opening the back-car door. He jumped in and, with an extra boost from my knee, made it into his familiar spot, riding shotgun like a human. He sat in the middle of the back seat with his legs resting on the middle hump, thrusting his massive head forward between my daughter and me. I patted him on the head, trapped in silent thought. *This is his last car ride, his last journey, and he's unaware, acting as if we were headed to one of his old haunts.*

I was inert…

"Let's go, Mom."

When we arrived at the vet, Spanky couldn't jump down from the back seat. In his attempt, he had wedged himself between the front and back seats. Two vet technicians rolled out a gurney and proceeded to pull him from the car. "Wait, wait," I cried. "You need to muzzle him because he's in pain, and he'll snap at you."

As they snapped the extra-large muzzle on my beautiful red dog, I looked at him and mumbled. "I'm sorry, Spanks, I'm so, so sorry."

Paxton averted her eyes and walked off into the street behind the car. They strapped him onto the gurney, and I walked beside him as they wheeled him into the room where a soft blanket lay amidst the glow of muted candles.

Paxton and I got down on the floor with Spanky. He was panting wildly and struggling to stand. "Please hurry and administer the first drug, please," I implored.

The sedative flowed through his body, his panting slowed and his body relaxed. I bent down in the child's pose, grabbed his gorgeous head in my hands and kissed him goodbye. Unbeknownst to me, Paxton took our picture and captured a moment that I will cherish forever.

When I walked through the front door of my new home, I stumbled over Tucker, who was awaiting our return. He looked up at me and saw the blue collar with the rabies tag dangling, and then he plopped back down, putting his head on his paws. I knew I would not be grieving alone.

Spanky was a once-in-a-lifetime dog, always there to help make lemonade when life gave us lemons. He had been my most loyal companion for twelve and a half glorious years and had fulfilled every duty of a family dog, always there for us until the very end.

Chapter 39

Sunrise, Sunset

ACCEPTANCE.

No photos were snapped, no congratulatory gifts or cards were given at this momentous rite of passage, planning for retirement. I didn't prepare myself or project that I would arrive at this marker—the final season of one's life. Where did all the years go? I never saw it coming. As I sat across from the Social Security administrator in my blue cashmere sweater, powerful emotions washed over me.

"I'm here just to shop, to see if I should, um, well, not really sure if it's the right time, if I'm ready," I muttered.

"Wouldn't it be easier," the young clerk replied, "if we could know for sure when we were going to die?"

When I left the cold brick building and climbed into my summer-heated car, a chill crept through me as I realized I was entering the final chapter of my life. *How*, I asked myself, *did all the chapters unfold so quickly?* Like a Russian nesting doll, the many chapters of my life were encapsulated—the engaging college girl, the hopeful bride, and the busy mother—they were all there tightly nestled inside one another. The outer doll was now full—full of wisdom and resolve, deriving strength from those intertwined lives.

I came of age before Roe V. Wade, integrated gender dorms, and Title IX, equal rights for women in high school and college sports. I was caught between two worlds: The *Leave it to Beaver* world of traditional family values and the emerging feminist movement of burning bras and equal rights. I was shaped by the angst of Vietnam and the restless Sixties generation, who were often reckless in seeking their own happiness. We were the Baby Boomers forging ahead with lives—some stuck in the past, some experimenting where no man had ever trod—but all of us were improvising as we became more and more liberated.

Liberation confused me. Trapped in two worlds, one based on traditional family values and the other based on the liberated world of too many choices, I sat frozen for thirty years. Sometimes the intertwined chapters of childhood—the innocence and goodness—collided with the realities and complexities of adulthood. Life knocked me down a few times and showed me things I never wanted to see, but I have finally gained a much-needed perspective.

We take our lives in chunks—in fragments of time—looking back with longing, wondering "What if…?" and "Why…?" We find it difficult to live in the present and accept what life has handed us. In our final season—our last chapter—we come to fully understand this universal truth: life is difficult.

Life is difficult because we want it to be easy. As young adults, we experienced life, but we lacked life experience. Much like learning a foreign language, we were not willing to conjugate the past to make sense of its power, or diagram the future to see its reward. Like all past generations, we had no Rosetta stone. Like many in my generation, I loved and parented by the proverbial seat of my pants. But now, this Baby Boomer has arrived. I have deciphered the complexities and cracked the code, finally becoming fluent.

Perhaps that is what landed me in my first writing class—a need to practice life, a need to become more fluent. I did not face life squarely until I was forced to by divorce. Then the floodgates opened, and I became the crazy divorced lady desperately seeking answers. Courageously, I dipped the quill in a bottle of anguish and wrote the words that burned on the parchment of life. I let the tears flow freely, dropping on the pages of my life—tears and words, a powerful elixir. Those mere words were my truth and savior. They peeled back the layers and found me.

With certainty, I know I have more days to travel in this life; I know I have more paths to explore and more forks in the road. For sure, I have more tennis to play, more holidays to share, and more roses to smell. As I sit on my deck, surrounded by a lush cornucopia of color with the sun dangling just above the horizon, I ponder this rite of passage into my twilight years. The passage into what, exactly, I really can't say, for there is no longer any protocol for old age. I can still wear my brightly colored skinny jeans, even in purple, paired with a turquoise cashmere sweater, if I choose.

I sip on my Pinot Grigio, petting my purring cat with my Shih Tzu at my feet, and I take heart in the choices I have made. Actually, I take even more heart that I finally figured out life *is* a journey of choices. We have been given free will. Would I have done things differently in some fragments of my life? Of course, but I am the person that I am because of my past, shaped by every person and choice along the way.

Time has washed over me and polished my humanity; the years have bleached the regrets and faded the scars.

I have a full season of life ahead— a bright future because I gave up trying to change the past. I have learned to live with the way things are now.

The dusk turns slowly into night where I am sitting in my Adirondack underneath a blanket of stars, still sipping and thinking. I am in awe of this fact: I have lived the life I have lived, and no one will ever walk quite the same path on Earth as I. I am unique.

The world will carry on, a very rapidly changing world, not as in tune with my rhythm anymore; stories I cannot even imagine will unfold; the sun will rise and fall, and the moon will wax and wane whether I am here or not.

With memories of my one-year-old namesake, my granddaughter, reaching up for my sun-spotted hand to steady her first steps, long forgotten sensations flood back...

To everything there is a season and a few cashmere sweaters. And each season holds treasures—like dogs and babies and maybe, *even*, a square oak table—unique to each person, yet every one of us is ultimately linked to the totality—like waves merging into the ocean—simultaneously distinctive and connected.

I lean back in my chair and smile.

Epilogue

No Stone Unturned

MY HEART HAD BEEN HOLDING ITS BREATH

Writing this cautionary tale has been a catharsis—a gift to myself. The power of telling my story and reclaiming my past has helped me move from shame to acceptance and from chaos to serenity. I no longer feel like I'm walking on a tight-rope, trying to keep my balance.

But I still had another leg to finish before reaching the end of my rope. My journey had stalled, and I teetered because of my inability, my lack of courage, to share my past with my daughter, Paxton. The *secret* sat like a stone in the pit of my stomach.

It was a day meant for renewal—and, simultaneously, a day meant for completion. It was a Saturday in late July; the hot weather was upon us, but the cool morning air had invited me to the garden. I stood in awe of the abundant, colorful landscape that I had helped create. Fragrant jasmine vines with their delicate white flowers climbed up wooden trellises and filled the air with a hint of sweet perfume. Twenty-five-year-old giant hostas, which I had saved from the Woodhaven house, hung like elephant ears over a stone pathway in my courtyard. Blood-red climbing roses in full bloom sprawled over the roof of a bench swing. *Better tame these*, I thought as I plucked a few dried, spent flowers. The feathery plumes of Astilbes, the sword-like arms of mature ferns and the ruffled circular leaves of Lady's Mantle all stood like sentinels, fighting for their turf. I had brought them from Woodhaven, so they were aliens in my new world called Dahlia Lane.

The sky, a baby-blanket blue, was filled with puffy animal-shaped clouds. Bees buzzed, flitting from one nectar-filled flower to another. Birds chirped, flying from one high branch of my cherry tree to a neighboring maple. I sat for a moment on my bench swing, marveling at nature's handiwork. A small sparrow swooped down from its perch and landed on the lip of my pedestal bird bath. Soon, it was splashing around with delight in the tepid bathwater. *A garden with all its complexity,* I surmised, *unlocks the fullness of life—carries endless possibilities. It's a healing place—my sanctuary.*

In this garden I should find peace. I have, but I need to live more gratefully, I told myself. *Paxton'll be home soon. I've missed her.*

Paxton was coming home for a week in between pet-sitting jobs. Over the past year, she had built her business so that she was only home a few days a month. I had grown accustomed to our arrangement, and truthfully, her absence allowed me to finish writing my book—sometimes, working into the wee hours of the morning with country western music blaring. Her absence also allowed me to avoid the inevitable: sharing my past.

Procrastination had seeped into my skin, lingering like an itchy soap. Every time she walked into our home; my stomach did flip-flops.

While I sat on the swing, engaging with nature's intricacy, the sun had climbed higher in the sky, chasing the puffy clouds away. A hush (except for an occasional croak from a frog under the deck) had settled over the garden as the heat drove the birds and bees into hiding. I sat facing my designer deck, waiting for Paxton. Lime green potato vines and variegated coleus spilled out of my planters. In one corner pot, fragrant basil plants surrounded a tall sunflower, which was bursting with yellow blooms. In the other corner pot, blue hydrangeas, which were supposed to be white, hung heavily on their stems, showing the surprise of nature. My handiwork, coupled with nature's wonders, lay before me in summer splendor.

My two cats had sought out their shady retreats in the courtyard where I sat gently rocking. One lay sleeping curled in a ball, hidden under the cascading Japanese maple that stood in the center of the garden. The other was sprawled on top of the deck table under a neon green umbrella. She squinted at me with her lemon-yellow eyes. Every once in a while, she would flick her tail and change poses, stopping to lick herself in contented pleasure. *Why can't I just enjoy and be in the moment? I sigh. Because you've let this linger…you've fallen into your old ways, letting fear control you. How do I begin? What will she think of me? Will she be angry like her sister had been? Will I lose her admiration and love? But…I can't go forward with…*

All of a sudden, Tom, the slumbering male cat, jumped onto my lap, startling me from my thoughts. "Okay, okay, I'll pay attention to you," I said when he nipped my arm.

At that moment, Paxton appeared on the deck.

"Hi, Mom." She smiled, taking a seat in one of the Adirondacks. "So happy to be home and to sleep in my own bed. Come sit down and let's catch up."

Always so positive, a bright light in my life. How am I ever going to tell her?

"Hi, honey," I rose from the swing, knocking Tom-the-cat from my lap. "I'm glad you're home, too. I've really missed you."

I took a seat in the other Adirondack and an hour flew by as we shared details from our month apart. We chatted about our lives like mothers and daughters do—and like roommates and best friends do; we discussed family, friends, food, tennis, our jobs, her dogs and how she loved the Standard poodle she had just cared for, our pets, how depressing the current news was, our opinions of Donald Trump, whether to bleach our hair, how hot the weather was, manicures, pedicures, eating fewer carbs, movies and books…

"Hey, Mom, you were right. I loved the book *The Girl on the Train;* I couldn't put it down. I stayed up really late finishing it, like 'til three in the morning…talk about dysfunction."

I laughed. "Yeah. I knew you'd love it. What are ya gonna read next?"

"Your book."

"Uh, um," I stumbled to find the right words—the right tone. "I'm not sure I'm ready…"

She peered over the top of her black-rimmed glasses. "Whad'ya mean? You've given it to all your friends. I've lived it…nothing I don't know about you and Dad." She paused. "You let me read some of the chapters, so I don't understand."

A jolt shot through my body. "I, just…well, something happened in my past that I'm not sure I want to share. I don't know, Paxton, maybe…" my words trailed off.

Her face turned beet red. "What? What happened? You didn't have an affair, too, did you?"

A wave of nausea washed over me. "No, Paxton, I had, uh, um… a baby when I was seventeen—a baby boy. You have to realize it was over forty-five years ago. I had to keep everything a secret; it was shameful back then."

Her face creased in confusion. "How? Why? What are you tellin' me? It doesn't seem like you…"

"I wasn't like…I was date-raped. But that wasn't in my vocabulary. He was my boyfriend, so…" I paused and took a deep breath. "I shouldered all the blame."

"Why, didn't you turn him in? I would've."

"Honestly," I explained, "it never crossed my mind. You've watched too much modern television—too many episodes of *Teen Mom* and that one with all the victims, uh…"

She interrupted, "*Special Victims Unit, SVU.*"

"Yeah, that one." I glanced sideways, not knowing how to proceed.

"So," she asked, "does that mean I have a half-brother? Is he alive? Do you know him?" She bent down and roughed up the cat. "This is a shocker, Mom."

"I know, I know. That's why, uh…well I just didn't want to burden you, but now it's out…" I hesitated, "Probably a good thing. I've agonized over telling you. You'll see when you read the book, but I'm scared. I don't want to lose you." I softened my voice. "I love you, and the last thing I want is to overwhelm you." I took another deep breath. "I went to a home for unwed mothers and gave my baby up for adoption. I did what I had to do. I've made peace with never knowing."

"How?" she flipped up her palms, questioning. "What did Nonna and Papa do? And Aunt Sue? And Uncle Joe? And…"

I jumped up from my Adirondack, ran in the house and grabbed one of my books. "Here, please read it, and all your questions will be answered, I think. After you read it, promise me you'll keep the communication and questions coming. In the end, this'll be really important for both of us, but it'll kill me if you clam up."

"Jeez, Mom, I'm almost thirty. I can handle it, though I wish you'd told me sooner—it's a big secret you've kept from me." She took the book and walked up the stairs to her room.

I stayed on the deck as the shadows lengthened and the cool, kindly breath of evening surrounded me. I sat waiting and worrying—waiting for the next set of questions, worrying about her responses to my responses. It would prove to be a long night; dinner sat uneaten on the back burner.

Before too long, Paxton came running down the stairs. "I knew it! I just knew it. I knew Dad had a secret child."

'*Ah, shit,*' a jagged shard of guilt sliced through me. "Oh, Gawd, Paxton, I never wanted you to know that. I forgot about the first chapter. I was so transfixed on my own secret. Please forgive me and don't hate your dad. It was so long ago…"

Tears welled-up in her eyes. "So, I have two half-brothers? Does Dad know him? Um, this is unbelievable. Really, so much to process. But I've always known somehow…"

I sighed. "Remember how you always said you wished you had a big brother? It used to cut me to the core." I hesitated and hung my head, afraid of her reaction. "In one fell swoop, you've been exposed to our secrets, forced to see our flaws, and now you have to reconcile yourself with the fact you have two half-brothers, and you'll never know 'em."

She turned and ran back up the stairs to her room, quietly shutting the door.

Chips of stars, glittering in the night sky, appeared, and a cacophony of frogs, croaking in the distance, serenaded me as I sat on the deck awash with guilt. *What have I done?*

Reluctantly, I pulled myself out of the Adirondack, turned out the downstairs lights and climbed the stairs to my bedroom, which was across the landing from Paxton's room. Yellow light slithered like a hissing snake from underneath her door. My heart thumped and I stifled cries because I knew my daughter's life was being torn asunder behind that closed door.

Traumatic events beyond her control would now alter her emotional landscape forever—and that's a long, long time.

Hoisting my Shih Tzu up on the bed next to Tom, who had already turned in for the night, I plumped my pillows, pulled back the covers and climbed between the silken sheets. Slivers of moonlight filtered through the shutters as I lay waiting—my heart was holding its breath. *I have wanted this to happen.* I stared through the blinds at the night sky, feeling conflicted and alone but, strangely, hopeful because I had dislodged a heavy burden—I was leaving no stone unturned in my landscape. The long-kept *secret* that had crawled under my skin and lodged in my soul had been pried loose— my grief at losing so much, at keeping so much hidden, had been freed. I rolled over and drifted off to sleep, allowing the Fates to guide Paxton's journey.

Long before the first gray streaks of dawn pushed away the inky black night, Paxton appeared in my room, full of questions. I was expecting her and snapped to attention.

"Mom, you told Megan? Why didn't you tell me? Were you ever going to?"

"Yes, Paxton, I was going to tell you, but I…I was waiting for the right time." I winced. "Didn't you read how sharing with Megan was the worst timing possible and a mistake of monumental proportions? One of the biggest regrets in my life." I shot up in bed. "In fact, it has badly damaged our relationship. Timing is everything. She hated that I dumped that burden on her. She feels it wrecked her college years."

"I guess you're right." She sat on the edge of my bed and began to pet the dog. "I wouldn't have hated you, Mom, it wasn't your fault. And I don't hate Dad. How will that help any of us? I do feel sad that I'll never get closure with him, though." A few tears slid down her cheek. "I'm sorry, Mom, that you had so many miscarriages and felt so alone."

"You and Megan wouldn't be here if I didn't have them. You certainly weren't going to be the fourteenth and fifteenth child, so I'm glad I had the miscarriages. Small price to pay for you guys. I can't imagine life without you."

"I finally read my birth story…"

"I've been hoping you'd do that…jeez, I gave it to you two years ago. See, you are a miracle and a survivor."

"Don't want to talk about it, but it does explain why I'm so fearful of doctors."

Tom had made his way from the foot of the bed and began to rub his head against mine. Paxton rested her head on the pillow and snuggled up with Tucker.

She sighed. "Um, that must have been so hard not to have Papa talk to you. He was, well, he was just my favorite person, I don't know why, I just loved him so. Can't imagine what you two went through. In the end, him asking about…" she stumbled on the words. "The… the baby, that really got me, Mom."

"Remember it was the 1960's, Paxton. Just how it was. I never held it against him. Just accepted the silence. And, yeah, he remained silent about it all for over forty-five years. So sad."

Empathy poured from my daughter like a fine wine. *Who has a daughter with so much compassion? She is an old soul, my sunshine,*

I reflected as the sun cast its earliest rays through the spaces in the blinds.

"I know this seems weird, Mom, but knowing all this helps me understand. Everything in my life, well, it just makes so much more sense. Dad's gambling, your crazy weak ways, Megan's anger... all just..."

"Family dynamics," I laughed. "We're not the first screwed-up family, and we won't be the last."

"I have one last thought and then I'd better get a few hours' sleep. Or try to anyway. It may take me awhile and maybe things will hit me, but anyway, I have to ask. If you'd kept, kept your..." she rolled her hands, again stumbling on her words. "Your son...would I be here?"

"Oh, Paxton, think about it. I would never have left Eastern Washington or met your dad. You wouldn't be on this Earth. You being here because of my choices is all part of the grand design of life. We can never look back to the future. You, me, Tom, Tucker—we're all meant to be here, on this bed—right now."

She smiled.

Acknowledgements

What a year! I began writing the stories in my book twelve years ago, and I finished the Epilogue in 2015. These stories were for my eyes only, and then I began to share with a few friends, then on a world-wide writing site called FanStory; I then ventured into a writing class where I was encouraged to "Tell my story or it would be buried with you." I have so many from these groups to thank for the encouragement and support they gave me; they nudged me forward into the Wild-West of publishing. Thanks, dear friends, thanks to the Marks, Ingrid, Sasha, and Bob (a many-time published author) from FanStory. Thanks to my Pulitzer-prize-winning writing teacher, Tom Hallman.

Thank you to my first editor Rama Devi who offered her amazing skills for a first-round of editing. She taught me to have a more active voice and to think more metaphorically and philosophically. Thank you.

When the Pandemic hit and I was about to turn seventy, my stories, which had been sitting for five years, began to speak to me to get on with publishing, and fate brought me Kate Allyson, my editor from afar. Since March 2020, we have worked together via the internet, gluing, cutting, and piecing my stories into a book. I fictionalized and agonized because my intent is only to help heal our wounds by recounting events many Baby Boomers may have suffered, but were never able to share. Kate led me to Eric Labacz, who designed the perfect cover that captures the essence of my story, an unraveling cashmere sweater. He designed it by just reading a few chapters, having one phone call and a few pictures of my old cashmere sweaters to go by…you nailed it. Thanks. Thank you also to Tamara Cribley, a graphic designer and professional formatter. The fonts she designed and the layout are so approachable and tie-in with the cover. All three of these professionals helped make publishing my book possible. I am grateful for you taking my hand through this process.

My sister and brother are my rocks. The common bond we have shared, and the support through all our ups and downs has brought us closer. I am eternally grateful and love you beyond measure. Thanks to my brother-in-law, too!

My wish for my ex-husband is health and happiness. We had our good times, and we share two beautiful daughters.

Lastly, I would like to thank my daughters who have enriched my life. I love you. My hope for you both is that you will find your happiness perched in your soul.

About the Author

Margy Adams lives in the Pacific Northwest. She privately tutors many subjects to a range of students. She lives with the last remaining cat from Spanky and his gang and continues to play tennis at a competitive level. Her love of books in all genres, and her belief in the healing power of words continues to keep her motivated as she enters her 7th decade.

Saying Good-bye to Spanky.

Made in the USA
Coppell, TX
23 July 2021